Girls

Savannah Avery

ISBN: 1512077925
ISBN-13: 978-1512077926

For my beautiful wife Kendra.

PREFACE

They asked me to talk. Everybody wanted me to talk. It's strange when you go from one extreme to another, when you're taught something is right and then expected to do the opposite. It wasn't until everyone was asking me to talk that I realized how silent I had been. It made me question whether I was always a quiet person or if I had become this way and if so when? I had learned to keep thoughts in my head, to think about every word I was going to say. The less you spoke, the more meaning the words you did say had. I believed that, even with all the people asking, begging, pleading, bribing, and even forcing me to talk. I had to think about my answers to their questions, had to work them so they came out correct and poised.

I wasn't covering for anyone, not for them and certainly not for myself. There was no point anymore. I stayed quiet for a long time, so I'm not sure what changed when the local news station asked me to talk. How was an under budgeted small-town news station any more important than my dad, or the police? They weren't. They called my dad, and asked if I could come in for a short segment to help "enlighten the world about what happened." When my dad quoted that it made me laugh, something I hadn't done in a while, regardless of what I chose to say the world would not be enlighten. For one, it was a local news station which meant that maybe ten percent of the people in a town of less than ten thousand would watch it.

But most importantly, no matter what I said or didn't say nobody would understand. They would never be able to understand the love we had for each other. I didn't even understand, not that I tried. Reason left with the girls. Even with all of this I told my dad I would do it, I would talk to the station about what I knew. Which, of course, was way more than they were expecting.

I'm not really sure what convinced me, all I knew was when I was sitting in that silver chair with the bright white lights shining in my face I was determined to tell every disgusting detail.

The women made me nervous- which made me uncomfortable- which made me feel guilty. Negative emotions are okay, it just depends on how you show them. Sadness could come off as beautiful, however being desperate or hysterical was annoying. Nobody wanted to be around someone who sobbed, but a young woman with tears streaming down her face was inviting. An invitation for comfort and love. Everything had to be thought out, even the way you felt. If you thought you felt some way you had to figure out why and how it could benefit you.

I tried not to fidget in my seat, I knew the cameras would be rolling soon and I wanted to appear calm and collected. If I seemed worried people might be more focused on that than my words. The women smiled down at me, which I suppose was a hint that we were going to be starting soon. She was pretty, but not in the way I was used to. She was pretty because she tried to be, she had on modern form fitting clothes that clearly were more expensive than she could afford, and her hair was slick and cut in a prefect angle barley touching her shoulder. I imagined her dreaming of being a big time news women in New York City. Obviously her dreams didn't work out. She was beautifully mature and sophisticated. We never utilized that imagine. While most girls our age were trying to look older we were trying to look younger, or I guess at least close to our age.

Whether we believe it at the time or not, youth is beauty. So instead of trying to use makeup and clothes to grow us up too fast, we avoided all of that and focused on the features we were born with. "Natural beauty is the firmest form of attraction" I could almost hear M's voice in my ears as I examined the news woman in front of me. M made sure we never wore a lot of makeup, that our clothes were simple and showed our best parts, we let our hair fall naturally and left it untouched.

Regardless of all of this, we were still gorgeous. She held our appearances up to such high standards, but expected us to be beautiful without trying. Sometimes I think that she picked girls like us because we were born naturally pretty, I can't believe the women sitting in the chair next to me would have been able to pull off what we did wearing no makeup. However, I suppose before I never would have thought I could be like those girls either. They were flawless, and I was average.

Kitty was the youngest, so she had the easiest time, she was too young to gain weight or have acne. Her body was slim and pale, her hair was long and matched her white skin almost perfectly. Her eyes were a stormy grey that always seemed like they were on the verge of tears. She was short and the outline of her bones were the only curves she had developed. She was the prettiest by far, she was also M's favorite. Opposite of Kitty was Katherine, her body was toned and her light brown skin accented her long straight black hair. M was everything she hated in other girls, she had the body of a woman, and she was tan and blonde and had blue eyes. But she had so much confidence in herself that you had to believe she was the most gorgeous girl in the world.

"You're really beautiful" were the first words out of my mouth to the news woman- she smiled politely at me again and started shuffling her papers. "I used to be pretty too. But not like you. I was a different kind of pretty" The woman was taken back, I instantly regretted saying anything but I felt like I had too. This is why I'm supposed to think about what I say. But I did think about it, I was about to tell her that I was one of them, and I knew she wouldn't believe me with how I looked now. It had only been two weeks since the police talked to us, but I wasn't the same person. My blonde hair had faded and was thinning out. I wasn't getting the sleep I normally did, so my eyes were red and puffy.

I was snapped out of my thoughts when the reporter cleared her throat and announced that we were about to start. My heart started to race and I looked down at my jeans. If I was going to say anything now would probably be the right time. I'm sure once the cameras started rolling they would start asking their questions- questions that I didn't have the answers to. Such as "were there any warning signs?" or "if you had to guess was M really the ring leader?". I looked up at the women and said "I lied. I didn't know anything about those girls. I only hung out with them a few times." And I walked off the set.

CHAPTER ONE

It started the last few weeks of my junior year, at least that's when it started for me. I had never dated anyone before, at seventeen most girls had at least one serious relationship under their belt but the chance never came up before. So when Mark asked me out I was surprised to say the least, sure we had sat together in class a few times, but we never even talked outside of school. We were sitting in the Chemistry class we had together when he leaned over and handed me a crumbled up piece of paper. I hesitantly took it, it wasn't like I was a nerd or one of those students who were aiming for an Ivy League school or anything like that, but the thought of getting in trouble terrified me. I quickly unfolded the paper and glanced down when the teachers back was turned.

"Will you go out with me tonight? Ice Cream? 7:30pm?"

I thought that he must have been joking, why would he want to go out with me? I had never been on a date before, so I didn't know how to respond. I didn't want to say yes, in case he had been kidding and I somehow didn't pick up on the joke. I didn't want to say no though either, because well he was kind of cute. I decided on looking at his face to see if maybe I could find a hint of sincerity. I folded the note up and put it in my pocket. I took a deep breath and glanced over my shoulder. He wasn't looking at me anymore. Great. I was going to have to talk to him face-to-face, because there was no way I was going to write him back without knowing if he was serious or not. I was not in the mood to be the butt of someone's joke, especially when this was a potentially huge moment in my life. I might have just been asked out for the first time.

I tried to relax and stare at the blackboard for the rest of the class, but I quickly realized I had no idea what I was supposed to be learning. My mind was racing while I was trying to focus on my notes. I shamefully admit that I even thought about us going to prom, and even having kids together one day. Pathetic, I know. I considered looking at him again, to see if maybe he would look back at me and I would be able to tell what his intentions were but I decided not to, what if he wasn't looking at me? People in the class would think I was some creepy stalker trying to catch the attention of a boy who was obviously more engrossed in his notes than me. No, it would have to wait until the bell rang.

This class seemed to drag on, I tried to not stare at the clock because everyone knows time goes by slower when you're counting down the minutes. At first I thought I wanted time to go by faster, so I could go up to him and ask him if he was serious. I could be able to have my first date, and that's massive! Of course I would want to know right away. But as thirty minutes left turned into ten my thought process shifted, what if I couldn't get his attention after class? What if he just walked out of the room before I could gather up my stuff? It's not like I could leave my stuff there and run after him, even if he was interested in me that would make me seem way too desperate. I didn't even have his phone number so I wouldn't be able to text him and ask, which would have been the easier option. I went from excited to 'why did he have to ask me out?' within minutes.

The bell rung and I got up casually and put my books in my bag. I decided that maybe I could avoid the situation, pretend I didn't read the note. If he wanted to ask me out so bad he could ask me to my face, and if this was all a big joke than I could avoid any embarrassment. I was finally starting to relax, when Mark came up next to my desk. His cheeks were bright red, like he had been thinking about the same things I was. I quickly wondered if my cheeks were as blushed as his. "Hey" he said shifting his weight from one foot to the other. "Hey, I got your note" I said, forgetting my entire plan. "Yeah, I mean we could just go as friends or whatever. The weather is starting to get warm so I thought maybe ice cream would be nice." I smiled up at him as his words ran together, obviously giving me the proof that yes, he was asking me out. And yes, he was just as nervous as I was. I agreed to go out with him, as long as I was allowed to have two scoops. He smiled at my joked and agreed. He gave me his phone number and he asked if he could walk me to my next class.

Everything people tell you about going on a date is true. I was so excited about my date that I tried on every single thing that I owned, I did my hair five times, re-did my makeup twice, and practiced walking in my new shoes that I bought specifically for that night. Yeah, I had ran to the store after school just to buy shoes for that night. I knew it wasn't anything fancy, we were just going to get ice cream. I even thought about how long it might last, and I figured with driving, and ordering the ice cream along with eating it and maybe talking for a bit afterwards, it couldn't last more than an hour. Mark had been very flirty throughout the rest of the school day, so I knew it was a real date even though he kept trying to downplay it. Still, it would only be an hour and I felt ridiculous making such a big deal out of it.

He picked me up a few minutes early, which was fine because I had been ready hours before. I don't know what I was expecting, but when I saw him wearing the exact same outfit he had on at school I was mildly disappointed. Maybe he didn't think this was a big deal, maybe he went on dates all of the time. I grabbed my bag, which had my weekly allowance in it just in case he wasn't going to pay for my ice cream, and walked out of the door and towards his car. It was small, and old, and dirty. But being as though he was only in high school and paid for this car with his after school job working at the local mechanic, it was pretty impressive.

He opened my door for me, which was sweet and kind of

corny. I sat awkwardly on the itchy fabric seat while I waited for him to walk around and get in the driver's seat. Looking around you could tell that a teenage boy owned this car, it smelled like old gym clothes and sandwiches, the rear view mirror had been scratched and was dangling by a wire, and I'm not positive but I think I saw an empty beer can in the backseat. I crossed my legs, and then realizing it showed too much of my thigh uncrossed them. "Ready to go?" he asked, I smiled and he drove off.

I'm glad the ice cream store wasn't far away from my house, because I was pretty sure the fabric of the seat was giving me an unattractive rug burn on the back of my knees. I probably should have went with the first outfit, which incorporated jeans rather than a mini-skirt. He got out of the car, and I didn't know whether I should wait for him to come open my door or just open it myself. The decision was made for me when I saw him walking up towards the ice cream store without even a glance back towards the car. Slightly disappointed I let myself out and walked up behind him. "What's your favorite kind of ice cream?" I asked trying to break the silence. "Huh?" he looked over at me, almost like he forgot that I was even there. "Ice cream...what's your favorite?" I asked again trying to hide the annoyance in my voice. Maybe he really did just want someone to come with him to keep him company, however I don't see why he couldn't have went by himself.

"Oh, I like vanilla." He said smiling down at me, he had the cutest teeth that were slightly crooked. He probably would have benefited from braces, but I thought it made him look friendly and childlike. "Vanilla? That's boring."

"What kind of ice cream did you think I would like?" he asked raising his eyebrow, he was flirting. He was definitely flirting with me. "I don't know, something adventurous like lime sherbet." He leaned against the wall and burst out laughing. "Lime sherbet is adventurous?" Okay. I guess that was lame. I looked down at the ground and blushed. "Come here." He said and I looked at him, "what do you mean?" I asked confused, we were standing in line to get ice cream, I wasn't sure where he wanted to go. He reached over and pulled me against him, it should have been a romantic gesture but our bodies didn't link up right. I ended up leaning against him with my head uncomfortably dangling off his shoulder. He didn't seem to mind though, he seemed perfectly at ease. Which was cute, and it made me feel special that he wanted to hold me. I was going to ask him right there if he liked me more than a friend, if this date was an actual date rather than just a couple of friends going to get ice cream together but I couldn't. What if I misinterpreted things? I've never been on a date before so how was I supposed to know what was and wasn't allowed. The extent of my love knowledge began and ended with romantic comedies and most people in those movies were older than me and I'm pretty sure their love life was way different than mine was supposed to be.

He bought my ice cream, I ended up getting the lime sherbet. We sat on a bench outside because it was starting to get warm. School would be out in a couple of weeks but it already sorta felt like summer. "You're beautiful" There he said it, I was so surprised that I almost coughed up my bright green ice cream. "Me?" I said stupidly. He grinned so wide that I could see almost all of his crooked teeth, yeah he was that cute. "Yes, I'm glad I finally was able to ask you to go out with me. I've been thinking about it for weeks now. All the guys on the team kept joking with me because I would always talk about you but I never told you how I felt." He said wiping the ice cream off my lips. "You told your friends you liked me?" I asked trying to hold back a smile of my own. "Of course. I think about you all the time, so of course I would talk about you." Okay. Now he was really flirting, it was obvious. "I want you to kiss me." I said quietly, half hoping he didn't hear me. He did though and then he grabbed my chin and pulled me close to him and kissed me, right there in front of everyone, with lime sherbet dripping off the cone and onto my white skirt, he kissed me. It was the best first kiss I ever could have asked for.

I thought about our date, and more specifically that kiss, all night. I laid in bed staring at the ceiling replaying everything that happened. I never even had feelings for Mark before that night, but now I was picturing having an actual relationship with him. He texted me the next morning, and it confirmed that the night before had not been a dream.

Mark- "Hey. I miss you"
Me- "Me too"
Mark- "Thanks for the kiss ;) "
Me- "You're the one who kissed me remember?"

Mark- "Only cause you asked me too"
Me- "I can't wait to ask for more things."

Woah. That was unexpected. I regretted typing that the second I hit send. I didn't even want to read his response. I turned my phone off and went downstairs. My dad had made breakfast like he always did on schooldays. That's how he was, always doing what he thought was expected of him. I guess making a giant breakfast every day before school, and letting me choose my own breakfast on weekends was what a prefect parent would do. I never knew who my mom was, I asked about her a few times but he brushed it off. I assumed she must have left us when I was too young to remember her. I think he tried to over compensate for her not being there. He read so many parenting books, and tried to be the prefect parent. He was never too strict, but he had rules. Rules that were barley enforced. Sometimes it was annoying. I don't know what I wanted from him, but it was different from what he was.

I grabbed a piece of toast and ran to the bus stop, even though I had my license my dad refused to buy me a car. Which I thought was ridiculous. What is the point of having a license if I can't even drive? He wouldn't even let me use his car, which made me having a license even more pointless. I probably could have walked to my high school, it was only a few miles from my house but I guess my laziness outweighed the embarrassment of riding the school bus with a bunch of freshman.

Once I got off the bus the first person I saw was Mark, he must have been waiting for me because I never see anyone I know hanging around the school buses. I waved at him, and hoped that the message didn't send somehow. "Hey sexy." He said grabbing my hips and pulling me closer to him. I was instantly self-conscious. He definitely got the message. "Hey" He kissed my cheek and walked me towards the doors to the school. "So, I was thinking we could go out again Saturday?" he asked "Saturday? Isn't that like tomorrow?" I asked, was this normal? We just went out yesterday, is this how fast relationships were supposed to go? As if he could understand what I was thinking he stopped and turned me around so I was facing him "Coco I'm gonna be honest with you right now, I like you a lot. And I kind of want you to be my girlfriend." I started back at him with my mouth open. "You want me to be your girlfriend?" He nodded while I replied with the lamest "Sure."

CHAPTER TWO

Being someone's girlfriend was a big deal. In just a week I went from never even being on a date to being in an entire relationship. I was happy though, he was cute and gave me a lot of attention. The problem I guess was that I didn't know how to be in a relationship, I wasn't sure how to act in that role. It's not like I had a group of friends that I could go to and talk about this with, I had friends at school if you could even call them that but I was never one to get close with other girls. Occasionally a group of people would invite me to hang out with them, and I would but it would never become a reoccurring thing. I didn't know how to make friends. It seemed so easy for everyone else, everyone at school seemed to have some group they hung out with but for some reason I could never find any. It never bothered me that I didn't have friends, however right then it would have been useful.

My new relationship was all I could think about, I probably should have just asked him what he meant by girlfriend. Did this mean he was going to tell everyone we were together? How often would we go on dates? And of course the biggest question of all, would we have sex? Even though I had never been kissed until the night before I knew about sex. I wasn't the shy type, or someone who wanted to wait until they found the love of their life. I liked to believe the only reason I was still even a virgin was because the opportunity never presented itself. I knew that if I was going to be in a relationship then it probably would involve sex, or at least some form of sexual behavior. I cringed thinking about those other acts. I decided I would text Mark after school and figure out what our new relationship would consist of.

Me- "hey"

Mark- "hey babe"

Me- "I have a couple of ?s"

Mark- "ok"

Me- "Were you serious about me being your girlfriend?"

Mark- "Of course"

Me- "What does that mean?"

Mark- "We go on dates, we kiss, whatever"

Me- "What about sex?"

Mark- " ;) "

A wink face, that's all he said. I didn't want to re-ask the question because what if I was supposed to know what that wink face meant?

Our next date was Saturday, and I wore a skirt again despite what happened last time. He took me to the ice cream place, again. Everything was the same, except that now he was all over me. The moment I got into his car he placed his hand on my thigh, making me rethink my skirt idea. When was I going to just wear jeans?

When we got our ice cream, we didn't talk much. He ate his ice cream pretty fast, and stared at me like he wanted me to finish mine. I was starting to hope all of our dates wouldn't be like this when he leaned in and whispered that I looked very sexy. "Thank you" I said with a mouth full of lime sherbet. Again, he placed his hand on my thigh this time it was cold from holding the ice cream though and made me jump a little. He moved his hand up higher until it was almost touching the rim of my underwear. I looked around, nervous that someone would see. I didn't want to tell him to stop because I knew he was just trying to show he liked me, I mean I was his girlfriend after all. I put my hand on top of his to keep it in place. "You done?" he asked while I was still taking the last few bites of my cone. "Um.. yeah" I didn't really want the ice cream to begin with. I threw the rest of it away in the trash can and he grabbed my hand and walked me back to his car.

Once in the car he drove to the local park, it was the only place in town that people could hang out. We didn't have a mall, and the movie theaters were very strict and only let you in if you were seeing a movie. He parked the car and turned towards me. "You are so sexy." He said, and before I could thank him, his hand was on my thigh again. I spread my legs, allowing him to touch me now that we were in private. "Are you a virgin?" he asked. I thought about lying, but what if he was the one? I mean, I know it was unlikely since he was the first guy I was with but still I didn't think I should hide that from him, so I nodded. At first I thought it bothered him but he leaned in and kissed my neck. I sat there not entirely sure what to do while he did that. He proceeded to take his shirt off and I sat back and stared at him, he wasn't fit, like at all. Since he was involved in sports you would think he had a nice body but he didn't. Seeing his body like that suddenly made me insecure about my own. If I was criticizing his body I'm sure he would be criticizing mine. I wasn't ugly, but I was kind of underdeveloped for a seventeen year old. He motioned for me to take off my own shirt and I did, then he leaned over again, this time hitting his knee on the steering wheel, and proceeded to kiss my neck.

This wasn't what I wanted my first time to be like, it wasn't even dark outside. If anyone walked by they would be able to see exactly what we were doing. I didn't want to tell him no though, now that we were this far, both undressed. He was obviously enjoying himself, maybe all he wanted to do was some heavy making-out. Those thoughts were instantly squished when his hand traveled all the way up my skirt. "Okay!" I said a little too loudly while scooting towards my door. I grabbed my shirt off the gear shift and pushed him away. "I'm sorry. I want to be your girlfriend and stuff. I don't want to do this though. Like here. Right now. I mean I'm fine doing it. Just not right now." I was rambling, and it wasn't working. He was pissed. "I'm sorry.." I said again, he sighed and smiled "It's okay". He started the car back up without putting his shirt back on and drove me home.

CHAPTER THREE

What's worse than knowing everyone is talking about you, is not knowing everyone is talking about you. I got off the bus on Monday morning and didn't see Mark anywhere, at this point I was thoroughly convinced that he broke up with me. He didn't text me after our date, not the night after, or the next day, or even that morning. I was starting to feel really good about not having sex with him, if he was willing to break up with me just because I wouldn't give it up in the front seat of his crappy car in front of everyone then he obviously wasn't interested in anything other than sex. I was a little upset that things didn't work out, and that I would forever remember my first kiss being with a jerk, but at least I didn't lose my virginity to him too.

I knew something was wrong the second I walked into school, but I still didn't put it together. Everyone, and I mean everyone, was staring at me. They weren't even trying to hide it! I pretended like I didn't notice them, but even that was starting to get difficult. I hurried to the bathroom to see if I had something on my face, or if I had a stain on my clothes. When I entered the bathroom there were a group of girls- probably freshman doing their makeup in the mirror. "What happened with you and

Mark?" the brown haired freshman with way to much lipstick asked me. "Excuse me?" I responded, looking over her head and into the mirror to check my face. The other girls she was with snickered and my defense went up. "What about mark?" I asked, suddenly sounding like the jealous girlfriend. "Are you guys still together? Because he told me you guys broke up, because of...well that incident. I only wanted to know because he is always flirting with me and I didn't want to help him like cheat or anything." I was so caught up in the fact that she just told me my boyfriend broke up with me, that I completely blocked out the mention of an incident. I grabbed my books and ran out of the bathroom, I felt the tears streaming down my face as I made my way to my first period class.

So, I had expected him to break up with me. What I didn't expect was for someone else to tell me we were broken up. I thought it would just go unnoticed, like we would never talk again. Or worse case, he would break up with me in person.

I sat in a seat in the back and opened up my book, maybe if I pretended to be studying nobody would notice me. Two guys who I knew were friends with Mark sat next to me, they were whispering to each other and stealing glances at me. Finally one of them said "You want to go on a date with me?" I kept looking down at my book, the tears were definitely there now. "No, don't go out with her. Mark says she's a tease." The other one said, they both laughed and high fived each other. Tease? How was I a tease? What the girl said in the bathroom came back to me, "that incident". No. There was no way Mark would tell people that I refused to have sex with him, and even if he did I wasn't a tease. We kissed like once, and I didn't touch him or anything. Maybe people were taking this break up thing too seriously. Considering we had only dated a few days, I know I was.

I made sure to find Mark as quickly as possible, I looked everywhere for him. I even walked the length of the hallway twice to try and see if he was there. I was able to catch up with him right before last period, he was standing in a group of guys. I stood in front of them for a couple seconds hoping he would notice me there and excuse himself, but when he didn't I cleared my throat and said "Mark!" It wasn't a question, but more of a statement. I even shocked myself at how brave I sounded. "What's up?" he asked like nothing had happened at all "Can we talk?" I asked the annoyance seeping through my tone. He nodded, "alone?" I continued. "Why? So you can ask to hook up only to tease me and leave me hanging? Nahhh, I'm good. You can go now." All of the guys around him burst out laughing, I felt the tears reappear. "I didn't ask to hook up." I stammered. "Read our text messages. You asked for it. Don't play innocent now." He then turned towards his friends and addressed them "she even claimed to be a virgin!" they were laughing so hard now that some of them had to lean against the wall to steady themselves. "I am a virgin!" I yelled way too loud, everyone in the hallway stopped and stared at me. I looked at Mark, pleading with him to stop this. "So...we aren't dating anymore?" I asked tears completely messing up my makeup. He rolled his eyes and walked away.

I was late to my last period class, I stood where Mark left me for a few seconds trying to get myself together. I knew my makeup must had been smeared, and there was no way I could hide that I was crying. I knew I would get made fun of in that class too, so I wasn't in any particular hurry to get there. The teacher could tell something was wrong so she just told me to take a seat and make sure it didn't happen again. I sat in the only seat available, the girl in the seat next to me smiled. I was hoping the teacher would just lecture about something and make us take notes, that way nobody would be able to say anything to me. I had it already planned out, as soon as the bell rang I would rush towards the door and walk home. I couldn't even take the bus anymore. Once I got home, I would fake being sick- a cold or something- and I could stay home for a week or so and by then things had to have calmed down. I mean, this was high school, there was always new drama. I actually started to feel better about this situation half way into class, I even decided I would email my teachers for my schoolwork so I wouldn't get behind. It would be a nice break from things, and I could forget that this ever even happened. That happy feeling left about as quickly as it came when the teacher told us to talk quietly for the rest of class, since she had some paperwork to do. I looked down at my notes, hoping nobody would notice me. There had to be better things to talk about than the drama of me not sleeping with my ex-boyfriend. How could anyone even be mad at me for that? I don't care what Mark said I didn't lead him on, and even if I did so what? I can decide who and when I want to have sex, and that was not the right time or place! What if I did sleep with him and someone saw, I probably would have been called a slut throughout school, but because I didn't sleep with him I was now a tease? There is no winning in high school.

Nobody was saying anything to me, which was good. I knew they were talking about me though, but I could handle that at least. People kept giggling and pointing towards me, perhaps because the teacher was still in the room nobody wanted to say anything too loud. I kept my eyes focused on the notes in front of me, and they were beginning to hurt. I could hear paper crumpling up next to me and instinctively looked over. The girl next to me was reading what appeared to be a note, I guessed that because it resembled the note Mark sent me only a few days ago asking me on our first date. The thought of that being not too long ago brought tears to my eyes. Luckily the girl wasn't paying any attention to me, she had an angry look on her face as she scanned the paper with her blue eyes. I couldn't help but stare at her, she didn't look like she belonged in high school. She looked older and the way she carried herself made it seem like she could care less what anyone had to say about her. Not that anyone ever said much, she was always with two other girls, who in complete contrast looked very young, too young to even be in high school. They kept to themselves, they seemed different than most people at our school, so it makes sense that they wouldn't try to socialize with anyone. They got attention from other people though, they were all beautiful, so most guys wanted to date them and most girls were jealous of them. I can't remember them ever having a boyfriend though, or even going to any school functions. Maybe that was the key to surviving high school, keeping to yourself.

She eventually folded the paper up and said in an unsettlingly loud voice "I don't do gossip, especially not through notes. If some guy didn't get laid even though he was promised it, I would guess that it had something to do with him and not the girl. I've turned down plenty of guys." And as if on cue the bell rang after the last word, everyone walked out of the classroom with their heads hung, as if they were the ones being bullied now. I was in such shock at how straight-forward she was that I didn't move from my seat. So much for my plan of rushing out of the room. I know she was probably trying to help, even though I couldn't figure out why, but her putting it out there for everyone including the teacher to hear made things feel way worse. I was so lost in my thoughts when she leaned over my desk and handed me the note that she was reading.

"Did you hear Coco didn't put out? Maybe you should make it up to Mark."

I re-read the note, just like she did, then I handed it back to her. "I'm guessing you're Coco?" she asked in a much quieter but just as strong voice as before. I kept looking at my notes but I nodded. "I'm M" she stated as if it was something I needed to know. I continued to ignore her, partially hoping she would go away and partially hoping she would make everything better. I could heard her sigh, and after a couple uncomfortable minutes of her standing over my desk staring at me I looked up and asked her "Why did you do that?" for a second I thought I caught a hint of annoyance in her eyes, what was I supposed to do? Thank her for making the situation worse than it already was? She didn't answer my question but instead said "Come hang out with me today." She said it like a statement, like she knew what was best for me. I wanted to say no, but how could I? I could pretend like I had other plans, but we both knew that wasn't true. So I agreed and she led the way out of the classroom.

She didn't walk besides me, or even talk to me while we walked out of the school. She walked ahead of me and I followed behind. It felt kind of strange, I barely knew her and she didn't seem like the friendliest person. She was interesting though, and perhaps that's what really drew me to her. She was everything I felt like I needed to be at that moment- strong and confident in myself. I never wanted to have a bunch of friends, I wanted to be left alone and happy. That's what I told myself anyway. High school always seemed so dramatic to me, people broke up and suddenly it was everyone's business. It was like everyone in high school was a celebrity and the paparazzi all in one. I know a lot of people thrive in that type of environment but I didn't like the attention. The whole act seemed fake and pointless, as soon as we graduated we would never deal with these people again, so why did we care so much about what they thought?

M didn't talk to me until we got out of the school, then she turned towards me and smiled "Aren't you going to ask me what my real name is?", I was so deep in my thoughts that I didn't know what she meant, she raised her eyebrows "most people don't think M is my real name, but it is." she continued. "Oh." I said and looked at my feet, why did she want to talk to me so bad? I started to hope this wasn't a charity act. She led the way towards the parking lot, again walking in front of me and not beside me. I didn't want to speed up incase this was how she wanted it to be, everyone at school seemed to hate me, maybe she didn't want anyone knowing we were hanging out. But, no, that couldn't be it because she just stood up for me in class.

She stopped so suddenly that I almost ran into her back, two girls stood in front of her. One was so small, and pale that you couldn't tell if she was beautiful or sick. The other stood against a car with her arms folded, she looked tough and angry. Looking at this group you never would have thought they were friends. They were so different in every way, the only thing that seemed to unite them was that they were so different than everyone else.

It seemed odd that neither girl asked who I was, I didn't know whether I should introduce myself or just act like I belonged. Luckily M was able to break the silence "This is Coco, is it okay if she goes to the park with us today?" she asked, looking more towards the angry girl than the small one. I never considered that they might not want to hang out with me, if they said no would I have to walk away? That would be uncomfortable. The angry girl nodded her head and started walking towards the end of the parking lot, M grabbed the small girl's hand and followed beside her. I stayed behind and eventually said "where are you going?" Only M turned around, but the other girls stopped where they were at. "We are going to the park, would you like to come with us?" M answered. I looked at M than back at the car they were leaning against a few seconds ago, I pointed to it without saying anything. "We don't drive, are you coming?" She said and continued walking.

I caught up with them and walked beside the angry girl, I was getting tired of the silence so I said "I'm Coco" realizing a moment too late that they already knew that. "I know." She said "I'm Katherine." I smiled at her, and tried to enjoy myself. At this point it seemed like these were the only people willing to talk to me without making some comment about me not having sex- again how ridiculous is that? "I'm Kitty" said the small girl, and her voice matched her appearance perfectly. It was soft and empty, even a little sad. It made me wonder what made her that way, she looked like she had friends that loved her. M was holding her hand and smiling at her. Even Katherine would look over at her as if she was protecting her from something. "What grade are you guys in?" I asked trying to continue the conversation. "I'm a freshman" said kitty, and even though she looked way younger than a freshman it still surprised me. The other girls were obviously older, why would they want to be friends with a freshman? "I'm a junior" said Katherine who seemed to be more relaxed now. "Me too." I said "what about you M? What grade are you in?" I was starting to notice that M took a few seconds before speaking I couldn't help but feel weird waiting for her to answer me. What were you supposed to do in that space? The other girls didn't seem bothered by this. "Technically I'm a senior, but I'll be dropping out soon." Wow, I was not expecting that. She didn't seem stupid, but she must have been if she was dropping out of school. I was beginning to think it wasn't a good idea to hang out with her, anyone who would drop out of high school was not the kind of person I wanted to associate with. "How old are you?" I asked, not that it would matter in the situation. "Eighteen." She said more quickly than last time. "I'm fourteen" Kitty chimed it, Katherine stayed silent, but since she was in my grade she had to be around the same age as me.

"Are you the same girl everyone was talking about today?" Katherine asked, I nodded. "What happened?" she asked but her tone indicated that she wasn't into drama either, she was just making conversation. "She doesn't have to answer that." M said. "No.. it's okay I don't mind" I said, I knew that Katherine wasn't trying to be rude, it actually made me happy to see her adding to the conversation. Maybe that meant she liked me. "I guess I was dating this guy, but on our second date he tried to have sex with me and I couldn't. I don't know why everyone is making a big deal of it, they keep saying that I was teasing him. I know we talked about sex, a little bit, but does that mean I'm obligated to have sex with him?" I realized that I was asking for advice. These girls who I tried to convince myself I didn't even want to be around where now the same ones I was asking advice from. M shook her head and she said "No" then Katherine said "You can sleep with whoever you want too." It made me happy to know that they understood how I was feeling, it seemed like everyone else thought I was supposed to have sex with him regardless of the situation. Maybe being friends with them wouldn't be so bad.

CHAPTER FOUR

Hanging out with them was boring, but a good boring. I'm so used to doing organized activities with friends, again if you could even call them that, like going to the movies. There was no doubt about what we would do doing and how long it lasted. Something about it having a set time when I could go home was comforting to me, I always seemed to hope that time went by fast when I hung out with people my own age. This was different though, we went to the park and just sat. We didn't even talk much, and I had no way of knowing when we were all going to go home. I guess of course I could have left whenever I wanted to, but that's the thing I didn't want to. I loved being alone but with people, I enjoyed the quiet and that there were no expectations. I knew I could do this every day and I understood why they did.

They said they liked the park because they didn't want to be bothered, it was the same park that Mark took me to, but I tried to forget that. I definitely didn't want to tell them and bring it up again. M laid under a giant tree and Kitty laid with her head on M's lap while M played with her stringy white hair. Katherine sat on the grass and started to smoke a cigarette. I always thought smoking was gross, and by the look on M's face she did too. They were quiet for a long time, and I wasn't sure what I was supposed to do. I wasn't even sure if a conversation would be appropriate since they all seemed content with the way things were. The quiet was peaceful, but it wasn't lonely like it would have been if you were here by yourself. "You're pretty." Katherine said breaking the silence, I assumed she was talking to me since she was already friends with the other girls and would have had many opportunities to tell them they were pretty. "Thanks" I said, and Kitty looked at me while still keeping her head on M's lap. She stared at me with her intense grey eyes for a couple of seconds, it felt like she was trying to look for something on my face. "Yeah" kitty said, as if she was answering her own question. "You would be prettier without all that makeup though" Katherine continued, I was shocked at her bluntness. Was that a compliment or an insult? "Oh.." I said still not sure. "Natural beauty is the firmest form of attraction" M chimed in. Her words had a rhythm to them, like she had said it a thousand times. Her eyes were closed but I could tell she was awake. Unlike Kitty and Katherine who continued to stare at me trying to judge every inch of me M didn't seem to care, she must have already had her mind made up about me. "Is that your real hair color?" Katherine asked, I nodded. I hated my long blonde hair. People asked if it was real all the time. "Pretty." Kitty said.

It had been about an hour, and I was started to get tired, not tired of being there I actually was enjoying it a lot, but tired from the long day that I had. Being emotional can do that to you. It can drain you of all the energy you have. I was thinking about telling them I had to leave when M said "We're going to go home now, but I would like to see you again." I nodded, because I would have really liked that too. "We do this every day after school, you can meet us in the parking lot if you want to come." She said, I was kind of confused why I had to meet her in the parking lot when we had the same class together at the end of the day. Why couldn't we walk together? My mind went back to thinking she was probably embarrassed to be seen with me after all the drama. "Coco?" she said "don't worry about what people are saying about you at school. You should be proud that you turned him down, he is the one who got rejected. Not you." And with that we smiled at each other, I had a new friend.

I don't know when I stopped having friends exactly, it was probably around the time that you had to start making your own friends and stop relying on your parent's to do it for you. I had always said that I didn't want friends, that it was the drama that stopped me. That maybe having friends was just too much work. After that day at the park with those girls though the truth was right in front of my face and I couldn't ignore it. I did want friends, I just didn't know how to make them. Maybe I had tried in the past, joining clubs after school and trying to start conversations in class. It would never work though. There was always a loneliness in my life. My life has always been boring and pointless. I lived a day to day existence, with nothing to look forward too.

Even though spending time with those girls made me feel better about the situation with Mark it also made me a little sad. I had experienced what it felt like to have friends, to have people to comfort you when awful things happen. I wanted to have that more than anything, and I had no idea.

CHAPTER FIVE

The next week was not very eventful, but it was so different. I had plans every single day with a group of girls that I barely knew anything about. I felt like I had friends, but at the same time I felt like they were complete strangers. And even though they were strangers, I felt completely comfortable around them, something I had never felt before with any other person. Being with them was different than what I thought a friendship would be. I mean, I was no expert but I had seen people with their friends and we didn't do any of the things they did. We didn't hang out at school together, we didn't eat lunch together at the same table, we didn't walk to class together, and we didn't talk during school hours even though M and I had a class together.

It was as if during school hours they didn't know me, but once school was over we were friends again, walking to the park. Even at the park we didn't talk much, which made it hard to get to know them. So far all I knew was how old they were (well besides Katherine, I still didn't know but I would guess about seventeen or eighteen), what grades they were in, that they had a different perception of beauty then most girls our age, that Katherine had an anger problem (she got mad one day when someone came up to her and told her she couldn't smoke in the park), and that Kitty was very attached to M. I suppose they didn't know much about me either. But I loved spending time with them, which was so unlike me. I thought that one of the main reasons I never had friends was because I wasn't the type. I couldn't stand hanging out with people from school. I preferred to be alone.

I noticed that I had changed a lot though in that week, I had stopped wearing makeup like Katherine had suggested. I still didn't think I looked prettier but I was insecure about what they would think, plus it made getting ready faster so I was able to sleep in now, which was nice. I also became quieter, not just with them but everywhere. I didn't speak unless I thought it was important, and the less I spoke the more I realized how much of what we said was unnecessary. I also stopped caring what people thought of me, I stopped wondering what people were thinking or saying about me and just focused on me. The only people I seemed to be worried about were my new friends.

Another thing that changed that week was that the drama went away, I knew that it couldn't have been because of what M said that one day, but it sure seemed like it. Nobody said anything to me anymore, and I hadn't even seen Mark since. It felt good not to be talked about, but something told me that even if I was still being bullied I wouldn't have cared as much. I felt protected knowing M was at the same school as me, even if we didn't socialize during school hours. Maybe because she stood up for me that day or maybe she just has a protective nature. Everything was going prefect, it was the last day of school so I wouldn't have to worry about high school for the next two months.

That was until I got off the bus, school had just started and I was walking into the building. That's when I saw him. Mark had either not been at school for a while or he was doing a great job at avoiding me because this was the first time I saw him since he broke up with me. I don't know what I expected to feel when I saw him again, was I supposed to feel sad that we weren't together? Probably not, the relationship was so short I never had time to figure out what my feelings were for him. I felt something though, he was my first boyfriend and my first kiss and I didn't want this to be how it ended. I knew we wouldn't be together forever, I wasn't that unrealistic. However I wanted my first experience with love to be something to remember not something I tried to forget. I didn't think I missed him, because I barely knew him and what I did know was that he was a jerk. I did though feel sorry for the experience, and as I was about to cry over him once again I saw that freshman girl who talked to me in the bathroom walk up to him and kiss him.

Yeah, she kissed him. In front of everyone, and it wasn't even a small peck on the cheek or even a school-appropriate kiss. It was a "yes-we-definitely-hooked-up-last-night-in-case-you-were-wondering" kiss. All sadness left my body and was replaced by an indescribable rage. I was so mad, I knew my face was turning red because of how hot I suddenly felt. The worse part was I just stood there, staring at them- probably with the angriest look on my face. I didn't care though, all I wanted to do was lunge at the two of them. I wasn't going to though, I was never the type to start a fight, even a verbal one. I'm just not that confrontational. I don't know how long I stayed there staring at the two of them- analyzing their every move. Coming to conclusion after conclusion and backing it up with facts.

She was prettier than me- that was obvious. They were a couple now- this wasn't a flirtation thing or even a hook up type relationship they were officially together. I could tell because she kissed him without any hesitation, if she was just a one night stand I don't think she would have been so forward and I don't think he would have been so accepting. They also held each other, like the way he tried to hold me when we got ice cream but it just didn't add up right, not like it did with them. Their bodies looked so happy snuggled up together. He likes her more than me- He wasn't looking at anyone else but her. He never looked at me like that. I couldn't believe that I was standing here staring at my ex-boyfriend, my first kiss, my first date, my first EVERYTHING loving up on this other girl. My thoughts went on and on, and I felt the tears stain my face. I didn't know who was looking at me, or what people were saying. I wanted to keep watching, even though it hurt.

So the bell rang, and I collected myself. If you call wiping your face with the back of your hand while tears still streamed from your eyes collecting yourself. I hadn't been wearing any makeup recently so I didn't have to worry about it all over my face.

The rest of the day was groggy, I went to my classes and didn't pay attention. All I could think about was them, how could he do this to me? Occasionally I would have little bursts of optimism- if he could move on so quickly he must not get emotionally invested in relationships and at least I didn't lose my virginity to him, those were quickly and violently crushed by the feelings of jealously, rage, insecurity and sadness. I was a mess, and I knew I must have looked it too. I didn't care though, what was anyone going to do to me? Make me feel any worse? I thought the bullying and the drama was bad, but this was on a whole different scale. I had never felt this way before, and feeling it made me sick. My throat felt like it had a giant rock stuck in it, and I knew if I talked even just a little bit I would burst into tears. My heart was pounding so fast, and my stomach felt heavy and empty. Was that what a broken heart felt like? I couldn't imagine people who were together for years and years and then broke up- it would be unbearable. This was unbearable.

For the first time since meeting the girls, I hadn't thought about them the entire day. I actually seemed to have forgotten all about them and our daily hang out routine until I arrived at my last period and saw M sitting at the back of the room. Even sitting there in the desk, she didn't seem like she belonged. She never did. She looked way too old to still be in high school, I mean it's not like she could have got mistaken for a teacher or anything like that, but she definitely didn't look like a teenager. I wondered when that would stop amazing me.

As soon as I sat down in a desk (away from hers, as

always) she got up and came over to me. She sat in the desk next to me and turned my way. She didn't speak, and I didn't acknowledge her there. I don't know why I didn't say anything to her. She didn't do anything wrong, this wasn't her fault at all. If anyone else was to look at us though they probably would have thought we were fighting. She sat next to me, looking for an answer. Then she put her hand over mine. She sat next to me for the entire class, and it made me feel better to know someone was there for me. I didn't feel so alone anymore. The hurt didn't completely go away though, actually it didn't go away at all. Her touch just made it much easier to deal with.

After class M walked with me, beside me, to the parking lot. We didn't even talk about it. Before I went into the class I thought that I wanted to be alone, but now I wanted nothing more than to be surrounded by them. Especially M. She was so wise, and I wanted her to wrap me in her arms and explain to me why everything was going to be okay. I felt, as if, having her tell me that my feelings of sadness and jealously were unwarranted would make them disappear. In that moment, with her walking by my side, I felt like she had that much power. She was strong and independent, and I wanted that. I wanted her in my life and I wanted to learn to be like her. I didn't want to care what people thought, I didn't want to care or feel anything ever again.

CHAPTER SIX

That day at the park was different than the rest, and it was better too. Obviously M already knew something was wrong, and the other girls must have figured it out by the way M was caring for me. In fact, for the first time she held my hand instead of Kitty's when we walked to the park. I know it sounds strange, friends holding hands. But she didn't feel like a friend, she never acted like a friend. She was something so much more. I don't know what you would have called us, I don't even know if there was a word for it. It wasn't a bad thing though, whatever relationship I was forming with her and these girls was something I never had experienced, and something that until then I didn't know existed. But now that I felt it, I never wanted it to go away. It felt like a bond stronger than friendship.

The air was colder than it normally was, even though school was officially over it didn't feel anything like summer. We sat in our regular spot, except I sat closer to M than I normally would. I rested against the sturdy tree and felt the cold breeze against my face. I took a deep breath and tried to talk without crying. "He left me, and I don't know why I'm so sad." I said, my voice breaking up as the tears inevitably broke through. Katherine looked like she felt bad for me and took out her cigarettes, and handed me one. "No." M said sternly and snatched it out of my hand and gave it back to Katherine. I thought I could hear Katherine mutter sorry under her breathe but I couldn't be sure. Kitty looked at me with her grey eyes, encouraging me to go on. "I never dated anyone before, so maybe that's it. I didn't even really like him! That's the worst part." Kitty nodded her head like she understood, I don't see how she could have though. She was so young. Katherine rolled her eyes, and for a second I thought she was annoyed with my story but I could see that she was irritated with him. She seemed like the type of girl who wouldn't allow a guy to break up with her. She was pretty tough.

"We went on two dates, and he wanted to hook up. On the second date. Who does that?" now M was looking at me, "I don't know" I said suddenly feeling insecure. "Tell us what happened" M said as she grabbed my hand again. "He asked me out in a note, in class. I didn't even know that he liked me. So, we got ice cream and I guess it was semi-romantic. It probably would have been better if I knew how to act on a date." Katherine laughed, and M shot her an angry look. I kept talking and pretended I didn't see it. "He even tried to hold me but it didn't work out very well." Kitty was nodding again. "So, then he asked me out again and I guess we were like dating at this point. I thought it was kind of soon.. right?" I asked but none of them answered me. Maybe they never had a boyfriend before either. "Then he tried to hook up with me and I didn't want to. It wasn't the right time, like we were in a car in front of everyone."

I looked at the ground, wondering if I should stop the story there. They didn't need to know that he broke up with me and told everyone I was a tease, but then again I guess M already knew that. Well, they definitely didn't need to know that he left me for someone else. "Then I told him I didn't want to do it, and I thought he was going to break up with me and stuff. He didn't though, he said it was okay!" I was getting angrier as the story went on. "And then he told everyone at school you guys were broken up?" M chimed in. I nodded. "I wouldn't have cared if he wanted to break up. I really wouldn't have. He didn't have to tell the whole school though!" After that I stayed quiet for a while, it's not like I was waiting for them to say anything. I knew they probably couldn't say anything to make me feel better, I just wanted to stop the story there. It was to upsetting to even say.

"Nothing is wrong with a tease" Katherine said. I shrugged. "No, seriously. What is wrong with a girl asserting her power over a boy? They want sex, and we have the power to either give it to them or not give it to them." I looked up at her, she couldn't be serious. My face must have showed shock because M interrupted Katherine and said "that's it?" I shrugged again. "That happened a while ago, but you were crying today." She didn't say it like a question, it was a statement, actually it was more like a command to tell the rest of the story. "I saw him today.." I said hoping that would be enough, or at least that they would ask questions so I wouldn't have to say everything. They didn't though, of course. Kitty was still staring at me, expecting more of the story. She looked like a child at bedtime listening to her parents read her a bedtime story. Katherine was smoking another cigarette, not completely engrossed in the story. M was looking at me, with a knowing look on her face. Like she already knew how this story would end. "He was with another girl. I think they're dating." I said finally. "What did you feel?" M asked. "Jealous." I answered instantly. "Why?" she asked, and I really thought about it. Why was I jealous? Because I didn't really like him, and I didn't want to hook up with him. "I don't know" I said. "yes, you do." Katherine said, and I could hear M sigh. "You cried today in school, you're crying now. There is nothing wrong with that, but you need to know why. If you don't know why you look like an idiot." M said, and the words stung. "I don't" I said desperately "I mean I guess I thought he liked me, not her." I continued, and once the words were out of my mouth I knew they were the truth. I wasn't sad because he left me, I was sad because it meant he never liked me to begin with. It didn't matter if I didn't like him, I liked that he liked me. Katherine was smiling at me as she took another long puff of her cigarette. "Power." She said as smoke escaped her mouth. Kitty nodded.

CHAPTER SEVEN

We stayed quiet the rest of the time, it was getting so cold that I didn't even want to be there. Finally M got up to leave "It's cold." She said as the rest of us got up. That was the strange thing about M, the way she talked. It was so calculated and simple. It wasn't even like she used proper English or anything like that, but her words were simplified and held such strong meaning. She spoke so seldom that hearing her voice felt like something amazing. She would speak and then return to her silence. She spoke to inform you, so you never felt like she needed a response. That's what made you think about what she said, instead of thinking about how you were going to reply. I wanted to be like that, I wanted to be like her. I wanted my words to have meaning, I wanted people to listen to me and think deeply about the things I said. I always seemed to be a rambling mess and I didn't know it before but it was a quality about myself that I hated.

"You can spend the night at my house if you want." M asked. At the time I thought it was funny, M didn't seem like the type to have a sleepover and I wasn't the type to go to sleepovers. "Okay" I said.

We walked to her apartment, which wasn't far from the park at all. I texted my dad on the way there and told him I was staying at a friend's house, he sent a quick reply letting me know it was okay. I hoped none of them saw me text him, I didn't want to seem like I had to ask my dad to spend the night. The apartment building was dirty, the parking lot had trashed scattered everywhere. The inside of her apartment was much better, it wasn't decorated much but at least it was clean. M walked into one of the rooms and told me I could put my stuff in there. I sat my bag on the floor and looked around the room. The walls weren't painted and there was nothing except for two beds. "Who do you share your room with?" I asked, I never thought that M had a sister. "This isn't my room" M said "Kitty and Katherine sleep in here. My room is across the hall. But Kitty normally sleeps with me." M continued "What?" I asked, but she didn't answer me. "Kitty and Katherine live with you?" I asked, thinking a better worded question might get an answer. I was right, she nodded. "What about your parents?" Now, I was really confused. "I live by myself. This is my apartment. Kitty lives with me and Katherine stays here during the summer while her parents travel." She spoke as if each word was a sentence. I understood not to ask any more questions, even though I had so many.

I walked back into the living room to see Katherine smoking another cigarette while Kitty started to clean. "Feeling better now?" Katherine asked. "A little, thanks" I said with a half-smile. Katherine came towards me and sat on the couch. The smoke of her cigarette was so heavy inside where there was no breeze to filtrate it. "You should accept what I said" she told me lowering her voice. "Accept what?" I asked, Katherine seemed different than Kitty and M. She was more like girls our age. She had an attitude problem for sure, and seemed to have no problem telling it like it was. "Power. That's what sex is all about. People think you have to be in a relationship to have sex, that it makes you a skank if you sleep with someone you're not in love with." She rolled her eyes. "I used to think that way too. I only had sex with my boyfriend." She put her cigarette out on the couch and leaned back getting more comfortable. "What changed?' I asked, even though I hated to admit it I was a little bit curious. "I learned differently. I had sex, and I wasn't in a relationship. I had no expectations. I didn't expect it to feel good. It actually hurt more than anything." Her face scrunched up at the thought of this. "I also didn't expect anything emotionally. I didn't like the guy and he didn't want me for anything more than sex" I stared at her for a moment then asked "So what's the point?" She sighed, impatient that I wasn't getting the point. Right as I asked M walked over. "What are you telling her?" M asked cheerfully. I was relieved to see she had gotten over my million questions. "I'm trying to make her feel better, she has the idea of sex all wrong." Katherine said taking a cigarette out of the pack. M shook her head and Katherine put it back. Thankfully. The smoke was beginning to fill the room. "There is no wrong way to have sex" M said "Some people have sex because they like the way it feels, something I never understood. Some people have sex because they are in love and think that having sex is a good way to show that other person you love them. Again, not something I have any interest in doing. Some people have sex for money, which a lot of people think is wrong, but it's your body and I don't see anything wrong with utilizing it. Money is good, but for me, I prefer to use sex to get what I want. It doesn't always have to be money- even though money is almost always involved. No. I want the attention."

What she had just said should have shocked me, repulsed me even, maybe I should have walked out right then. She had sex to get what she wanted. I didn't exactly know what she meant by that, but I could tell that was not how I wanted to be. I had never had sex before, and I just had my first kiss a few weeks ago. Now I was around these girls who talked about sex so freely. They didn't look at it as something complicated. I was disgusted, but also intrigued. I knew I didn't want to do that, but I also knew that I wanted to know more.

"How?" I asked. "How what?" Katherine answered. "I mean, why I guess. Why do you think of sex that way? How do you do it?" I stammered. Kitty made her way over into the living room but continued to clean as if we weren't talking. "Sex for me is exciting. I love being able to control a guy. When I'm having sex, and I know that I don't want the guy for a relationship, all the power is in my hands. I can either go through with it and have sex or I can deny him and leave him wanting me. Having that power feels like nothing else." Katherine said passionately you could tell she meant what she said. "However, sex is different for everyone" M interrupted "No one way is the right way. You just have to find what's right for you" now she was directing her words towards me. "What's the right way for me?" I asked looking at them. They seemed to have all the answers.

"Well it seems like obviously sex in a relationship didn't work out too well for you" Katherine laughed and I looked down. Here I was not even able to have sex with a guy who liked me, and took me on dates and these girls were able to hook up with whoever they wanted. They didn't even seem like skanks either, skanks let guys have the power. They sleep with whoever would want them, these girls are choosy. They only want certain guys, it's not about the sex. Even M said she didn't like the way sex felt and Katherine said it hurt when she did it. It actually started to make sense.

"I didn't like that I didn't have a say." I said and Katherine nodded. "I..I think that I didn't want to do it then, you know, in front of everyone." I continued, Kitty had now came and sat on M's lap. "Maybe you're like us" Kitty chimed in. She must have been listening to the conversation, even though she was preoccupied. "What do you do?" I asked again, this time M looked at Katherine. "Normally M finds us the guys. It's easier that way, she knows what we like and stuff. We meet somewhere, and we have sex with them. It's on our terms though, we control what we do and what we do it for. We leave when we want too, and we decide whether we ever see them again. They have no control. It's all about us." Katherine said as she played with the pack of cigarettes in her hand, I could tell she wanted another one. "You said it hurt though" I questioned. "Yeah, it does. A lot. The first time, but after it's not that bad" Katherine shrugged it off like it was nothing. She seemed tough though, maybe she could handle that kind of stuff better than most people.

"It's not about the sex though." M said "It's about the feeling. When you saw Mark with that other girl what did you feel?" she asked, knowing my answer already. "Jealous" I said. "Did you feel jealous of him or jealous of her?" She asked. "Huh?" I said surprised by her question. Of course I was jealous of him. I didn't even know that girl. "Were you jealous because she had him? Or were you jealous that he choose her over you?" I thought about it. She was right. I wasn't jealous of him, I was jealous of her. I wanted to be the girl he wanted, even though I didn't want him. "Yeah." She said "But besides jealously, what else did you feel?" she pressed on. "Insecure" I answered honestly. "Exactly, you let a guy control the way you felt. He made you feel ugly. He made you question everything. Girls should never let a boy make them feel that way. Especially a girl as beautiful as you." She ran her hand down my face, and I believed every word she had said. I had never felt beautiful before, I knew I wasn't ugly but beautiful had such a strong meaning. I wanted to be beautiful, I wanted to be independent and careless. I wanted to be like them. I could be like them. They had already accepted me into their group, I didn't know if this was an invitation but I thought it could be. "So, I could do it to?" I asked, hoping they wouldn't reject me. "Of course" M said "You can go with Katherine tomorrow and watch her. To see if it's something you could do." I kind of expected Katherine to be uncomfortable with the idea but she wasn't. She seemed excited. Maybe that's how it was with them, maybe everyone else was wrong.

We stayed up the rest of the night talking about our experiences with boys. I had little to tell of course, but I told them about my kiss with Mark. They didn't gush over it like most girls would have, but they listened deeply. I loved talking to them, we talked for hours and the conversation never got dull or empty. Katherine did the most talking, and I was starting to really like her. She had a hard exterior but I could tell she had a fun personality. Kitty was quiet but when she did speak it was usually something funny rather than insightful. Sometimes I could tell she wasn't even trying to be funny, which made the whole thing even more hilarious. M spoke when she felt like she had to correct someone, or if she was asked a direct question. It was almost like she was a monitor for our conversation, but it wasn't like we had to censor anything. We could speak freely but know that if something was said wrong it would be fixed. I fell asleep on the floor, when I woke up Katherine was asleep next to me but M and Kitty were in the living room. I could hear them talking as I woke up, they both were laughing and it sounded like they were having a pretty long conversation. That surprised me because both of them seemed very quiet, I still didn't understand either of them.

"Hey" I said to Katherine, her eyes were open but she looked very tired. "Hey" she said back and got up. "Comfy floor huh?" she said and I smiled. Katherine was easier to understand. "Super comfy!" I said sarcastically. "What time is it?" I asked "I have no idea, probably early." Katherine said. We both got up and headed towards the living room. Kitty was laying on the couch and M was sitting on the floor, they both stopped talking when we walked in. "Hey" I said, Katherine took her spot on the other side of the couch and I sat next to M on the floor unsure of where else to go. "You still want to go with Katherine today?" M asked, I looked at Katherine and agreed. "Okay, well you have to leave in about an hour. So you better go get ready" M said to Katherine and with that Katherine got up and went back into the room. I sat there uncomfortably, I only had the clothes I wore to school the day before plus I was sure my hair was a mess. I knew I wasn't going to be doing anything, but I also didn't want to look awful. Katherine was beautiful, her skin was flawless and she had the prettiest smile. "You look fine" M said, I never understood how she knew what I was feeling. "It's not about you anyways" Kitty stated from the couch. I didn't know if that was supposed to be an insult or not. Maybe she was trying to make me feel better. "Okay" I said.

CHAPTER EIGHT

We walked to the boy's house, it was just me and Katherine. I thought about how Katherine might have felt walking here alone, would she have been excited or nervous? Maybe she didn't feel anything at all. Maybe sex was made into a bigger deal than it really was. I started to wonder if this was something I could really do, if I was this kind of girl, if this was even something that was okay to do. Being with them made me start to question if I wanted to be the kind of girl I was, or if I even knew what kind of girl I was. Perhaps I needed them to finally be myself.

Katherine didn't look any different than normal. I'm not sure what I was expecting- high heels and a mini skirt? That wasn't them. She was wearing jeans and a t-shirt, but she was gorgeous. Before we left, M looked her over and said she looked fine. "You're quiet." Katherine said "You guys are always quiet." I said jokingly. "No, Kitty and M are always quiet. I actually talk a lot. M is always getting on my back about it. She thinks when people talk too much there words become meaningless." Well that explains a lot. "Do you agree with her?" I asked, not wanting to insult M in front of Katherine. "Sometimes" she said.

The house wasn't far from M's apartment, once we arrived I realized I knew nothing about this guy. I started to think that maybe I hadn't made the right decision, what if it was someone I already knew? Before I could tell Katherine I didn't want to do it anymore she walked right into the house. She didn't knock or anything. I followed quickly behind her, my feet moving before my mind told it that it was okay. The house was small, and Katherine made her way towards a bedroom. It was obvious that she knew the boy, and that made me feel a little bit better. She stopped outside of the door "You can stay outside, or you can come in." she said and I could tell she wasn't going to wait long for a reply. "I want to come in" I said. This time she knocked and a tall, college boy opened up. I don't know what made me think he was in college, but something about him definitely said college. His shirt was already off, so it was clear he knew what was happening. "Who's this?" was the first thing he said, pointing towards me. He sounded more excited than bothered by my presence. "Don't mind her, this is about us. She's just going to watch." Katherine said, in a tone of voice I wasn't used to hearing. It was softer, like she was trying to be seductive. That anger and attitude she seemed to always carry with her disappeared when she saw him. "Sit on the chair" she told me motioning towards the chair by the wall. Ironically it was lined up perfectly to the bed. Katherine started to kiss the guy, but he didn't touch her. She grabbed his hair then ran her fingers down his chest. He had a really nice body. He was tan and looked like he played sports or something- why did he have to have meaningless sex? Couldn't he get a girlfriend? I tried to make these thoughts go away, I was trying to understand the girls meaning of sex and why it was different from everyone else's. Why it could work for me.

Surprisingly I wasn't uncomfortable, even when things got a little more heated. I knew what sex looked like, and I knew what happened during it. Seeing it in person, right in front of your eyes, was not much different than knowing how the act works. I started to see what Katherine meant about power, she was completely in control. He didn't make one move without her telling him too, and he was focused on nothing but her. They definitely didn't seem like a couple, even though it was give and take. She was giving and he was taking. It was not equal. She was right, it was powerful.

When they were done, I didn't even try to act like I wasn't staring. I'm pretty sure they both knew I was. I was impressed, and by the smile she gave me she knew it. She got her clothes on, and he tried to pull her closer to him. "Come lay with me for a while" he said sweetly. "I can't, we have things to do today." He groaned and said fine, he still had a huge smile plastered on his face. He looked pathetic, he could have at least pretended he wasn't completely infatuated with her. Someone as sexy as him, who I knew could get any girl he wanted, was lusting for Katherine. She was loving this. He reached under the bed and pulled out some money and handed it to her, she put it in her pocket without saying anything. "Thank you" he said. "Come on" she said to me and I got up and waved bye to the naked boy on the bed.

Walking back to M's apartment I couldn't believe what I had just done. Sure, I didn't have sex with the guy but I watched it! It was exhilarating. I had never seen a boy be all over a girl like that, he wanted her and she could care less.

"What are you gonna do with the money?" I asked, she shrugged and said "It's not about the money, remember?" and she was right. Who cares about the money? I wanted that feeling, I wanted to feel what I knew Katherine felt. I wanted to be wanted. Not by some stupid high school boy, but by sexy college boys. I wanted guys to want me so much that they would give up their money to be with me. "I want to do it" I said "I can tell" she said laughing "you were staring pretty hard" I felt my face go red "I'm sorry.." I began "No, its fine. That was the whole point. I'm not sure if M will let you do it but it's worth asking. I'll let her know you were okay with everything today." She said. "Katherine?" I asked hesitantly "what if I can't do it? You were impressive in there, and I'm not sure that's something I can do." Katherine looked at me seriously and stopped walking. "I didn't know much of anything before I met M, she will teach you. It might take some time, but it's worth it. You gain everything you saw today, but you also gain us."

When we got back to M's apartment they both were dressed up, not completely dressed up, but they wore dresses and their hair had been done. They actually looked better when they didn't try. Maybe that's what Katherine meant when she told me I would be prettier without makeup. I knew they must have been going somewhere, so I went into the room and got my bag. It would be better to leave then to be asked to leave. I had such a great day, I was happy to have friends like them. They were the type of girls I wanted to be like. So, even though I was upset that they had plans without me I had to accept that we still weren't very close.

I walked out of the room and saw M combing Katherine's hair, Kitty was sitting on the couch looking small in a big yellow dress. "Where are you going?" M asked without looking up from Katherine's hair. "I was going to go home, it seems like you guys have plans." I said, trying to sound relaxed and not at all bothered that I was left out. "Katherine's parents asked us to meet them for dinner." She said. That made it seem more okay, they were going to see her parents. Of course they wouldn't invite me, her parents didn't know me. "Do you want to go?" M asked. I didn't know how to answer that. If I said I wanted to go, which I did, would I sound desperate? But if I said I didn't want to go I might offend them. "Yeah, if you're okay with it." I answered failing at my attempt to sound like it didn't matter either way. "Go into the room, and pick out a dress. You and Katherine are about the same size. Make sure it's appropriate, and please comb your hair. It's a mess." She ordered.

I hastily went into the room and looked through the closet, it wasn't hard to pick out Kitty's clothes from Katherine's. Katherine tried to dress like Kitty, but with her muscular body it didn't have the same effect. A shirt would flow over Kitty's skeleton body where it would be fitted on Katherine's. Not to mention the quality of Katherine's clothing was far better than Kitty's. The material in Kitty's clothes was lightweight and loose, while Katherine's was strong and well-made. It was interesting seeing the differences in the girl's attempt to be alike. I picked out a long orange dress, and it fit me well.

We walked to the restaurant, and it was very far away. When we arrived, her parents were already waiting for us. They were both dressed in business attire and had on very expensive jewelry. We must have all looked very odd compared to them. Even Katherine didn't look a thing like them. Her parents had money, which went without saying. Katherine didn't seem like the rich-girl type. I had seen those types of girls at our school, the ones whose parents make a lot of money working in the city. Those girls showed off their wealth whenever they had a chance, they wore designer clothes and talked about extravagant parties and vacations. They were flashy and obnoxious.

Hello Katherine" her mother said in a deep voice, Katherine forced a smile. "M, Kitty" she said nodding them towards their seats. Katherine didn't sit next to her parents but instead sat between Kitty and M, I ended up next to her father. "And who is this?" her mother asked now looking at me. "I'm Coco" I said and offered my hand up in a hand shake, her mother smiled at my hand but didn't shake it. "How is my daughter doing?" her mother asked M, which I thought was kind of strange, why wouldn't she just ask Katherine who was sitting right across the table from her? "She's doing fine, school is out and I'm sure all of them are excited about that." She was referring to me, well to us.. Katherine, Kitty and me. "I'm glad to see there haven't been any more problems" her father spoke up, he had a scratchier voice than the mother. "Okay. Can we just eat?" Katherine asked and M shot her a warning glance. "I'm just saying, we can't have any more fights. You have given us a lot of trouble to clean up." He continued. M was nodding her head in agreement "I know she has been hard to deal with but she is doing much better." She ran her fingers through Katherine's hair. "I don't know why it took you this long." Her mother muttered. Poor Katherine, she had just gotten here and they were already criticizing her.

The rest of the dinner went on like this, they would talk about Katherine to M like she wasn't even there. Kitty and I both sat quiet and still unless asked a question. I had never felt younger than I did then. M was only a year older than me, but she acted like an adult. It was annoying to be looked at as a child, especially when I was a year away from being a legal adult like her. There was a comforting element about it though, I didn't feel like I had to impress her parents like I normally did when meeting someone's parents. I knew M had the entire situation under control. She always did.

The walk home seemed longer than the walk there. It was getting dark and I was so ready to go to sleep. Nobody said anything but I assumed I would be staying at M's apartment again. I hoped I would remember to call my dad and let him know. M and Katherine were doing the most talking, Katherine was complaining about her parents and M was letting her, even though M wouldn't say anything negative or agree with what she was saying. She probably knew that Katherine had to get her frustration out. Eventually she stopped and it became quiet again. "You got in fights?" I asked cautiously. "I used to, I had a really bad anger problem before." I nodded, "why?" I asked, but she didn't say anything. "If your parent's travel all the time, why do you stay with M? Why don't you go with them?" I asked. M gave me the angriest look, and Katherine didn't answer.

CHAPTER NINE

When we got to the house we all went to sleep, I slept in the room with Katherine and Kitty slept in M's room. Before I fell asleep I wanted to think about everything that happened that day. I felt confused, only a few weeks ago I was going to school and coming home, there was no excitement and I was so alone. Now everything changes all because of a stupid boy. It didn't make sense. I was sad and insecure, because of him. But I was hopeful and happy because of the girls. I tried to think back to before we went on that date, was I happy? Or did I merely think that everything was fine when really I was missing out on so much?

I wondered if it was them, if they were so special and so compatible with me that we were all supposed to be close, or if it was all timing. If they happened to be there when I needed someone. If I would have met them before Mark would I be intrigued by their lifestyle or repulsed? I didn't know the answers to those questions and I wasn't even sure that it mattered.

"Are you awake?" Katherine spoke softly from the bed across the room, she couldn't see me in the dark but I turned towards her anyways out of habit. "Yeah..just thinking" I said "About what?" she asked me. "A lot" I answered. She didn't say anything for a few moments. "I think you would be good" she said and at first I wasn't sure what she meant but then she went on "you're pretty, but it takes more than that. It's about having that need, and I can see you need something." I think she was right.

"What made you do it?" I asked unsure if she would answer, it was kind of a personal question. "My parents have a lot of money." She began, that was obvious after today. "I was spoiled, and I got whatever I wanted. I had a bad attitude though, they never wanted to spend time with me. I did things for attention, you know smoking and fighting, that kind of stuff. It got me attention too, from the school and other students. Not my parents though, whenever I got in trouble they spent less time with me. I didn't learn though, and eventually the fighting became less of an attention thing and more of a frustration thing. I needed someone to love me and take care of me. I acted like I was so tough and older than I was, but that's not what I needed. One day I got into a fight at the park, it was bad. M was there with Kitty and saw the whole thing. After the fight she came over to me, I was crying and didn't see her there. She told me that fighting was pointless, that it made me look weak. You know M, and her advice. Something about the way she talks you know, it makes sense. She always says the right things at the right time. Anyways, I was still mad and part of me was annoyed by her getting in my business, but the other part was relieved that someone cared. We started hanging out in the park, and I stopped fighting as much. At first I thought me fighting less would get my parents to show me attention, but it didn't." I could hear the pain in her voice, and wanted her to stop. I didn't want to hear her cry, and I was sure that it was inevitable.

"Well, M could tell that I wasn't happy, so she went to my parents. Without telling me or anything, just went to the house and talked to them. I don't know what was said but M came back and told me that I would be staying at her house for a few months. She told me that my parents loved me but that it was my fault that they were distant. She said I had to earn their love back. It's been about a year since we became friends. I guess I'm still trying to earn it. I stay with them during the school year, but I spend all my time with M. I only go there to sleep." She sighed.

"How did the sex thing start?" I asked trying to change the subject. She laughed "I was dating this guy at the time, we had been together for a while but it was a typical high school relationship you know?" I didn't but I didn't say anything. "We had sex when he wanted it, and it was always boring. I would go to school and hear him brag about it to his friends, which was you know uncomfortable. Well, one day he came over to M's place, while her and Kitty were out. We weren't supposed to do anything but we ended up making out on the couch and M walked right in and saw us. Like I know she isn't my parent or anything, but she kind of is the closest thing I ever had to one so I was completely freaked." I couldn't picture M caring much about someone having sex, and especially not someone making out, that was nothing. She did have a lot of parent-like qualities and she definitely was in charge but sex didn't bother her. That was evident within the first few hours of meeting her.

Perhaps she wasn't like that with Katherine.

"She got really mad and told the boy to leave, and I knew she was going to yell at me and instantly my attitude came back. I would never fight M, no matter what, but I was ready for an argument." She continued. She didn't talk to me for days after that, and it was horrible. Until then I didn't know how much M meant to me. I wanted her as my friend, but I knew that already. What I didn't know is that I wanted her for so much more. I needed someone to love me and take care of me. I needed someone to protect me." She said, and I could tell that she needed a parent. "Anyways, I apologized to her. She told me she wasn't mad that I was kissing him, she explained her opinion on sex and how it could be used for things other than love. She told me she was mad that I was lowering my standards, she said that she thought I was worth more than what that boy was giving me. And all that time I thought she was mad because I hooked up on her couch. Nobody ever talked to me the way M does, I would do anything for her. I love her." Again, she ended the story there but I wanted to know more.

I had to know more about this girl who was once in the same spot that I was in now. "What else?" I asked. "She told me that if I was going to continue to be with that boy that I had to tell her when he was coming over. She also gave me tips on how to make sex more you know enjoyable for me. She taught me how to make him want me." I knew Katherine wasn't in a relationship now, at least I didn't think she was. "What happened to the boy?" I questioned "We stayed together for a while, the sex did get better, and he wanted me more which was good. The bragging to his friends didn't end though and he was still just a high school boy so there was only so much he could give me. I saw the guys that M brought around, and I started hooking up with them. Sometimes they would even pay me, and I gave the money to M. You know because I lived there and stuff, she paid for everything. She would always be so happy with me whenever I could get money for us. I didn't even feel bad about being with other boys while I was dating him. I mean he didn't seem like he wanted to be with me forever or anything like that, so why did it matter? We broke up because he took up too much of my time, time that could have been spent with M or other boys. I could tell M liked that I broke up with him. So, that's how I got here." She sounded happy, unlike the beginning of her story that was filled with such sadness the ending sounded accomplished.

What was I doing before? Was I really happy then? I thought back to my life before them, it wasn't that long ago but it felt like it was. Did I have everything wrong? What could my life be like with them? I could be happy like Katherine, I could change and be loved and accepted. I could be beautiful. I could be acknowledged by boys, and never have to worry about feeling the way I felt when I saw Mark with that other girl.

"I think I want to do it." I said, hoping Katherine was still awake "You can't think, you have to know." She said "Once you start it there may be no way to change your mind." I didn't know what she meant by that. "You could always just try it out on your ex-boyfriend, you know like I did." She said after a few moments. "Mark?" I asked surprised. "Yeah, do what I did today on Mark and see how it makes you feel. It will be easier to deal with. Since, you know, Mark is someone you already know." She said. Our conversation ended there. I didn't know what else to say to her. I fell asleep thinking about her.

I woke up to M playing in my hair. She was already dressed, and the light colors of her clothing contrasting with her tan skin and blonde hair reminded me of summer. The window was open too which filled the room with thick hot air. "Hi" she said when I finally opened both of my eyes. I wanted to roll over and go back asleep, but I also wanted her to stay there with me. "I talked to Katherine" she said and that woke me up for good. I didn't know if I should be mad at Katherine or not. I shouldn't have been surprised, as close as they all were I couldn't expect her to keep anything private from M. "Okay" I said and she stopped playing with my hair "Do you want to have sex with Mark?" she asked. I shrugged, I didn't know if I did or not. "Do you want to be like us?" I nodded, I knew for sure that I did. "I think it would be easier to start with someone you know." She was right.

CHAPTER TEN

Over breakfast M gave me advice, Katherine sat there looking so pleased with herself. I guess this all was happening because of her. Kitty, as usual, sat quiet and looked sad. I thought that maybe she looked sad because M wasn't giving her attention. I was becoming close with Katherine, and even though M was distant we still were developing a relationship, but me and Kitty had nothing. She never opened up with me like Katherine did, and she had nothing to give like M. She didn't even seem close with Katherine, which I found a bit strange.

"Don't try to be older than you are" M said first, "a lot of girls think dressing sexy and wearing a bunch of makeup makes them seem older. It doesn't. When you pretend to be older than you are, you actually look younger. For example, if you tell someone you're 25 but you look 18 they are going to know you're lying. You know why? Because if a 25 year old looked 18 they would lie about their age and say they are younger. The only people who want to be older are the ones who are young. Be proud of your age. Youth is beauty. Most boys actually want someone younger than them. If you're with a high school boy don't pretend to be twenty, that will intimidate them. If you're with a college boy, don't pretend to be his age, he will know you're lying and it will make you come off as immature." Katherine was nodding her head at everything M said. It made sense though, and I wondered why I never thought about it like that before.

"Don't wear makeup or do too much with your hair. Natural beauty is the firmest form of attraction." She had said that before, when Katherine told me I would be prettier without makeup. "But doesn't makeup make you look prettier?" I asked, and M shrugged "Yeah, I suppose. If you're ugly. But you wouldn't be sitting here if you were ugly."

"Don't dress too sexy, wear whatever you feel comfortable in. Expensive clothes, revealing clothes. None of that matters. Boys don't care about clothes. If you show too much of your body you have already given away something. This isn't about them remember, it's about you." She continued.

"You remember everything Katherine did yesterday?" she asked, and I nodded a bit shy that I had to admit that I watched her. I could see Katherine trying to suppress a grin. "Don't try to do what she did, she has experience and you don't. Just make sure you are in control, don't let him do anything you don't want to do." She said "That worked out well last time." I said sarcastically. "No, last time you apologized. Last time, you made him think that you couldn't do what he wanted. This time, if it happens, make sure he knows that it's because you don't want to. Make him feel bad, make him think he did something wrong, make him feel insecure, make him apologize."

She sounded so fierce, I knew what she meant though. I saw the way Katherine had complete control. That was the main reason I wanted to do this, Mark made me feel so bad about myself. I had never had low self-esteem until he came into my life. Well, I guess I had low self-esteem before him. When he asked me out, I thought it was a joke. Why would a guy wanting to go on a date with me have to be a joke? Why wasn't I worth a guy's attention? I was and M and Katherine had proven that to me. They told me I was beautiful, and even Mark wanted to hook up with me, but I had turned him down. I just went about it the wrong way. I wanted that to be the last day I would ever feel insecure, I wanted to be proud of how beautiful I was. I would listen to whatever M told me to do and I would do it. I wanted to feel what Katherine had. What M had.

"Should I text him?" I asked when breakfast was over, Kitty was in the kitchen doing the dishes and M was about to walk into her room. "That would probably be a good idea" she said without even turning around. I sat on the couch next to Katherine, "What should I say?" I asked. "Tell him you're willing to give him another try." I laughed "what?" Katherine said "Seriously, you should say that. It makes it seem like he was the reason you freaked out last time." I nodded and took out my phone.

Me: "I'm willing to give you another try."

It took him a while to answer, and I was beginning to think it wasn't a good idea until I heard my phone ring.

Him: "Try what?"

I looked at Katherine, unsure what to say but she motioned for me to go on. I knew what to say.

Me: "I'm bored, so if you're not busy I was hoping we could hook up."

Wow, that was straight-forward.

Him: "Okay"

Okay? Seriously? That's it? I sighed and showed the message to Katherine, who rolled her eyes.

Me: "If you're gonna be like last time, then nvm."

Now, I was being straight-forward. I didn't care though, he

was making me mad.

Him: "I won't ;)"

I told Katherine that he put a wink face and she burst out laughing, we both sat on the couch laughing at him for a few minutes. It felt good, maybe this would work.

Me: "I'll meet you at the park"

CHAPTER ELEVEN

I stood at the same spot that he took me the last time, my confidence drained the closer I got. Katherine asked if I wanted her to go with me, but I said no. I thought it might have been weird with her there. Plus, she was so amazing the other day that I didn't want her seeing how bad I was going to be. Katherine let me borrow some of her clothes, and although she was almost my size the clothes didn't fit that well and I hoped he wouldn't notice. I saw his car pull up into the parking lot, he didn't get out of the car so I walked over and got in. "Hi" I said, my voice smaller than I had hoped it would be. "Hey" he said, almost as if it was a question. I couldn't back out now.

I thought about talking to him, and explaining everything. I wanted to ask him if he was dating that girl, ask him why he choose her over me. I realized something then though, he wasn't with her. Well, he might have been dating her but right then he was with me. He choose me over her. If she found out what he was doing, she would probably have broken up with him and that was a risk he was willing to take for me. All the insecurity I felt when I saw them together washed away and I felt confident. At that moment I got on top of him and started making out with him. He didn't kiss me back at first, I think he was surprised at my forward-ness. Then he kissed me, and I felt his hands move towards my lower back. I grabbed them and moved them up, I stopped kissing him and gave him a smile that let him know that I knew what I was doing.

Katherine was right, it did hurt, a lot. I tried to pretend like it didn't, but I'm not sure I succeeded. I made a note to myself to ask Katherine if it hurt every time like that. If so, I wasn't sure it was something I would be doing anymore. When we were done I made sure to act like it was no big deal, like I hadn't just lost my virginity to a guy who tried to ruin my high school reputation a few days ago. "So, are we like dating now?" he asked. I looked at him like he was an idiot. "No." I said very clearly. He seemed insulted. "Why not?" he asked "because, you are a jerk and I don't date jerks." I said while putting my pants on, which by the way if you have ever tried to put pants on while in a car it is not easy. "So you just give it away to any guy?" he asked, sounding meaner and reminding me of when he left me standing there in the hallway after breaking up with me. Could he have been a bigger jerk? He breaks up with me and tells the entire school I'm a tease but now he's accusing me of just giving it away? There is no winning with boys. If I hadn't met M and Katherine and Kitty I would have been crying at this point. However, they had taught me that this wasn't about him it was about me and I wasn't about to let him ruin this for me too. "I give it away to whoever I want too. I'm starting to think allowing you to have a second chance with me was a mistake. I must admit you were better than last time though." He stared at me for a moment, and I was hoping my fake confidence would be believable. He then gave me that goofy grin of his which now looked pretty stupid. "Do you need a ride home?" He asked and I shook my head no.

The whole walk home I felt great, it also helped that after a couple minutes he texted me and told me he had a great time. I couldn't wait to tell Katherine about it, I wanted to give her details and ask her questions. I knew she wouldn't feel uncomfortable, we were friends after all. When I got to M's house I didn't know what I wanted, did I want them all to be waiting eagerly for me to come back, or did I want only one or two of them to be there casually not concerned about what I just did? Part of me wanted to gossip, and spill everything that happened, but I knew they weren't like that. They were always so calm, like nothing ever excited them. I had thought a lot of times that it was only because we weren't close yet, that that side of them would come out later in our friendship.

I knocked on the door, and Kitty answered. She said "hi" and let me in, I saw Katherine on the couch smoking a cigarette and although she looked like she was pretending not to care I could tell she had been waiting for me. "Hey" she said with a huge smile on her face, okay maybe Katherine was the gossiping type. "Hey" I said much quieter than her, my face reddening. She grabbed my hand and led me towards the bedroom, she didn't even invite Kitty to come with us. I felt bad as Kitty sat on the floor and played with the hem of her pants. She seemed like she was always left out unless M was around, and even then she seemed more like a child hanging around with her mother than a friend. I wanted to know more about Kitty but now was not the time to ask.

"Sooooooo.....?" Katherine began. "So what?" I asked, I don't know why I was playing this game, we both knew what she was talking about and I wanted to spill as much as she wanted to hear. Katherine playfully nudged me, "Okay okay!" I said giving in "We did...it" I said. Katherine gave me a look, a look that meant 'that's-really-all-you're-gonna-tell-me'. I closed my eyes and smiled, "Okay..like it was good. Well, I liked the way it made me feel. He was different. He was all over me." She clapped her hands and smiled even bigger than before, if that was possible. I went into more details, becoming more comfortable with her as the conversation went on.

You think you know how someone is, and you can be completely wrong. That's how I was about Katherine, out of all the girls I was obviously getting closest to her. Not by choice, I'm sure if I was able to pick which one I wanted to be close with I would have easily picked M. She was the one I wanted to be like, but she was so intimidating. I kept telling myself that getting close to her would take time, Katherine was the girl that was convenient. She was around most of the time, physically and otherwise. M wasn't around that much, she seemed to always have somewhere to be. And even though Kitty was around almost as much as

Katherine she wasn't there. She would stay quiet, only chiming in occasionally. Sometimes I thought that was her trying to be like M, only speaking when she thought it was important, but she failed miserably if that was the case. Her voice didn't have meaning or power like M's did. In fact, when she spoke it proved how small and weak she was. I don't know how she never got made fun of in school, she was not only a freshman but also completely different than everyone else. I would have thought that even the freshman would have made fun of her, because she looked way younger than fourteen and she acted younger too. I supposed M being so close to her was why nobody messed with her, even though M kept to herself anyone could tell she wasn't someone you wanted to get off on the wrong foot with.

That's what I thought about Katherine too, I thought she was mean. She had an attitude, and acted like she didn't care about anyone. She was not someone I would have approached, ever. She was gorgeous, of course, but I thought she was one of those girls whose beauty is crushed by her personality. Out of all of them, I thought Katherine would be the one I had problems with. If you would have asked me the first day I met the girls who I would have clung to I would have said M. That's where I was wrong. Katherine was not like she seemed, maybe it was because I now knew her story that she opened up, or maybe because she could tell I was becoming like them and she had made that transition only a year earlier. We could relate to each other, and we both still held on to our teenage selves, something that we could let out only when we were around each other.

A few nights later, I was asleep in bed with Katherine. That's how it was, we would all sleep in random places. Sometimes, like tonight, Kitty would sleep in our room and I would share a bed with Katherine, sometimes we would fall asleep on the couch, it didn't matter where Kitty, Katherine, and I slept. M always slept in her room though, sometimes Kitty would sleep in there with her but never Katherine or me. I woke up to someone playing with my hair, I knew it was M by the strength she used to separate my hair. She was gentle and loving but the act also had a purpose. Sometimes I felt like she would start out playing with my hair to show affection but then would get caught up in removing the knots. I turned over and opened my eyes, "Yes?" I asked non-sarcastically. "Can we talk?" she asked and I nodded. I carefully got out of bed so I didn't wake Katherine up and I walked barefoot into the living room where M had sat on the couch. She motioned for me to sit beside her and I did. I was still half-asleep but it looked like M hadn't gone to bed yet. She still had her clothes on from the previous day. I wanted to ask what time it was, but I didn't want her mistaking that for me being annoyed that she woke me up.

She stared at me for a moment, then said "Do you know how much you mean to this group?" that was not something I was expecting. I shook my head no, and she sighed. "Everyone has a purpose here, and I love these girls with all my heart. There was something missing though, someone." I didn't know what to say, so I just looked at her. "I don't know if you want to do it" she continued "I want you to do it though." She was looking down, was she about to cry? "I know you are better than that girl I met a few weeks ago, crying over some boy. I know what you were meant to do." Her voice was steady letting me know that she was definitely not crying. "We are a close group of friends" I smiled at the word friends. "I want you to be in that group, but you have to be able to understand us and do what we do." I wasn't sure what she was talking about, I guessed she meant having sex with guys. "Why?" I asked. "Why does it matter that I have sex with guys?" After I said it I hoped that's what she meant. She looked up at me, and ran her fingers through my hair. "That's who we are, it's what we believe in. If you have to ask why, then maybe I was wrong about you." She kissed my forehead and got up. "No, M." I said. I didn't want this moment to be over, she was giving me attention. One-on-one attention, she was being so kind and open. I didn't want it to end. It did though, she closed the door to her room gently, not like she was mad though, which kind of made it worse. I ended up sleeping alone on the couch that night.

CHAPTER TWELVE

I woke up before everyone else. When M left me on the couch the night before I was convinced that the next morning I would make her believe that I was like them, that I could do this. It was something I wanted more than anything. If that was true though, why did I take all my stuff and walk out the door?

I went home, and went to bed but it didn't feel right. I wasn't tired, and I felt lonely. My mind went to wondering if they knew where I went, if they even cared. I'm sure Kitty wouldn't, she would just go with the flow like she always did. Katherine might have cared, maybe she would ask M where I was but I knew what would happen if she did; M would dismiss her, and tell her to forget about me, because M knew why I left.

I looked at my phone, I had a ton of texts and I opened them hoping that they were from them but I knew they weren't. Matter of fact I never gave them my number, and I never saw any of them with phones, except M. She had a cell phone that she rarely used. I couldn't even picture Kitty having a cell phone and texting. She was so anti-modern that seeing her with technology would look out of place, not to mention she looked like someone entirely too young to even have a phone.

The texts were all from Mark, which made me happy for a second. I thought about yesterday- the day we hooked up, for real this time, in his car and it made me smile. It wasn't the most pleasant event, definitely not how it goes in the movies (or how Katherine did it). However, it worked! He had texted me things like "I miss you" and "Can we go out again?" that one made me laugh, go out like we would go for ice cream again or something. He even sent longer texts apologizing for how he acted and telling me he broke up with his girlfriend. Wow, I knew I wasn't that good in bed..er car? But he was over here acting like he had fallen for me. Is that all it took to make a guy want you?

I thought about calling him for hours, I still had no romantic interest in the jerk who tried to make the whole school hate me, but I wanted a distraction. I wanted to be around someone who wanted me. I knew that it probably meant having to have sex with him again, something I wasn't entirely looking forward to, but it would be worth it to hear him tell me all the things that he said in texts.

"Hi beautiful" was the first thing he said to me when he picked me up. That word seemed to be said a lot recently. I got in his car, and to my surprise it actually looked cleaner than it ever had before. I wondered if he took the time out to clean his car. Pathetic. "Hi" I said, trying to sound calm and like I didn't care, and once I saw that goofy smile on his face I realized that I didn't. I didn't have to ask him where he was going, we both knew it was the park. He pulled into the same spot he had the past two times, I wanted to ask him if he had any creativity but I resisted. I was in a bad mood, that's why I was here. I shouldn't take it out on him and ruin it.

I had expected him to start kissing me or touching me or at least looking at me to start things but he didn't. As soon as he turned the car off he sighed and said "Do you still like me?" That caught me off guard and when I said "What?!" a bit too loud, I could see the hurt on his face. "I...uh I just meant like do you like me? Cause we hooked up, but you didn't like seem interested or whatever." He was rambling, and it was cute.

I got in the back seat and took my pants off. He just looked at me, and that kind of made what was supposed to be an attempt at being sexy not so sexy. "Are you gonna come back here? Or am I gonna be naked for nothing?" I said in a playfully annoyed tone that I hoped he would pick up as flirting. He climbed in the back seat with me, leaving barley any room and kissed me.

It wasn't better than the last time, but his compliments were. He told me how beautiful I was, it seemed like he was complimenting me every couple of minutes. I could tell he was enjoying himself sexually even if I wasn't. That was okay though, because the attention he was giving me was enough to make me happy. When we were done I quickly got dressed like last time, not wanting anyone to walk by and see me. When I was almost in my pants he asked me to be his girlfriend again. I wanted to say yes, even though he was a jerk and even though I had come to realize I wasn't attracted to him at all. I wanted the attention he gave me to be a daily thing, I wanted to be loved by someone, I wanted to never be alone again. That's when I realized I didn't have to be with him to get all those things, they were already offered to me, last night by M. I told him I didn't want anything other than sex from him, and I couldn't tell if he was upset or turned on again.

I walked back to M's house, I wanted to see them. I needed to see them. I was scared it was already too late though. I knocked on the door and Katherine answered, she looked like she didn't want to see me. "Hi" I said and my voice sounded sturdy. She rolled her eyes but I knew Katherine, and her having an attitude wasn't a big deal. Kitty was sitting on the couch with M. M looked at me, like she expected me. Kitty ignored me. "Can I come in?" I asked after a couple of seconds of standing in the door way. Katherine groaned and moved out of the way, letting me in. "Hi" Kitty said, she was obviously unaware of the tension going on. "Hi Kitty" I said, happy for any sign of welcome. Katherine leaned against the wall with her arms folded, her face was scrunched up and it looked like she was waiting for an explanation.

How had I gotten here? Katherine was being a bitch, for no reason. She probably didn't even understand what was going on. M was acting like she knew I would be back. And Kitty was ignoring everything. These girls were weird, these girls were nothing like me.. they were nothing like each other either. They were all different. But they made a group, with one thing in common. The ability to control boys. I still wasn't sure I had that ability, but I knew that I wanted it. I could learn, I could stay my own person. I could learn parts of each of them and make myself into something better.

I don't know what came over me, a rush of confidence. Maybe it was from seeing Mark, or maybe it was all just making sense. I had let these girls control me, and this whole thing wasn't about giving away control it was about taking it. I had been insecure, when I was supposed to be learning confidence. I had let them have their secrets, when I was supposed to be their friend. "I want to talk to M. Alone." I said. The words shocked even me. Kitty quietly left the room without a look at M or a word to me. That was who she was, always doing what she was told. It must have been an easy life. She never had to worry about doing the wrong things, because choices were always made for her. Katherine stood firm in her spot. She looked even angrier than before, but I wasn't afraid. That's who she was, always getting mad, always acting strong. Kitty and Katherine, completely different but they fit so well into the group. "Go to the room Katherine." M said and Katherine went. Apparently I was learning my place. Above Kitty. Below or equal to Katherine? M gave me the meanest look I have ever gotten, it was a different kind of mean from Katherine's. I was afraid of M. Not that she could physically harm me, Katherine was stronger than M. I didn't want to upset M, I wanted her to love me and I wanted her to let me be hers. "What?" she finally said, probably getting irritated by the silence and the fact that Kitty and Katherine were in the other room waiting for this conversation to be over. I was below M, way way way way below M.

"I'm sorry." Were the first words out of my mouth. She nodded, like she had expected such a generic answer. She didn't seem impressed. If this was going to work, I had to open up. She had given me the chance to do it the night before, where it would have been easier. We were alone, Kitty and Katherine weren't listening from the bedroom like they probably would be now. M was in a better mood then, she was loving and sweet but now she was critical and annoyed. Being a part of this group meant doing things that wouldn't be easy. That I had already figured out. This would just be one way to show M what this meant to me. "I'm scared." I said, and it seemed like she was listening more closely now. "I don't know how to do this, but I want to learn. I want to be better than I am now." She nodded, like she had heard what I was saying before. "I love you, and Katherine and Kitty" I said, and I meant it. Even though I wasn't sure my feelings for Kitty yet, she was a part of them and I loved her for it. This got M's attention, and she turned towards me. "Let me be in your group." I continued, hoping this would be all I had to say. M's silence told me I had to say more. "I had sex with Mark today, I was sad and I called him. We had sex and I got what I wanted from him." She looked amused. I couldn't tell if she was impressed or if she was mocking me. "You said your group needed me, but I think I need you guys more." She nodded, like she agreed with me and that made me feel discouraged. She agreed that I need them more than they needed me. "Let me live with you this summer." I thought I heard a gasp coming from the room, but I could have been wrong. M didn't seem shocked though, all she said was "Kitty, Katherine you can come back now." The door opened and I saw Kitty sitting on the bed, waiting and Katherine, who had obviously been by the door listening walked back in. Kitty got off the bed and found her place on the couch. "Go home." M said. Katherine looked mad still, but a trace of disappointment was on her face and that made things better. Kitty didn't seem like she cared one way or the other, maybe she didn't even know what was going on. She put her head on M's shoulder.

"No." I said. And M looked at me, and I could feel the anger. Katherine didn't look mad anymore, she looked like she didn't want to be there, and Kitty moved to the other end of the couch. It seemed like they felt her anger too. "I want to be with you guys. I want to be a part of your group." I was begging. "I love you guys. I messed up. M..I'm sorry. Nobody has ever loved me like that." As soon as I said it I wondered if it was true, or if I knew that it was what she needed to hear. "I need people like you. I can learn. What do I have to do?"

M got up and even Kitty looked afraid. There is something about seeing someone else's emotions that can really affect yours. Like when you see a tough guy crying, even if you don't know why it can make you sad. That's how I felt looking at Kitty. When I saw Kitty's face, I knew that I had messed up. Big time. Kitty was neutral, in everything.

Sometimes she looked sad, but mostly she seemed neutral. Nothing made her happy, nothing made her mad. She seemed so unaware of everything that went on that it was easy to forget she was even there. But now she was aware, so aware of M's feelings that she was scared, and that made me scared.

I backed away as M moved closer, a few seconds ago I wanted nothing more than to be close to M. In her arms, having her welcoming me back to their group. But then, I wanted nothing more than to be as far away from her as possible. She got close to my face and said softly, but not in a whisper. "You have one more chance Coco. I like you, and that's the only reason I'm letting you stay. You need to learn to respect me though. I love my girls but to be one of my girls you need to act like it. Ok?" She looked me up and down, with so much disgust I thought I would never feel pretty again. She walked back towards the couch and Kitty's face was calmer now. "By the way" she said loudly enough for the girls to hear "please don't mention Mark anymore. It's not impressive that you can get laid by a high school boy."

I slept in the room by myself that night. Katherine slept in the living room, which hurt. I don't know if M told her to or if she just decided to on her own. I had left her without saying goodbye, I can understand why she was upset. She had been the one who wanted me to join them in the first place. She had been the one I was closest too, she had told me so much about herself and I was just throwing it away.

It felt good to be back, but it also made things difficult. I wanted to prove to M that I was worth it. I didn't know how though, Kitty took care of all the cleaning before the place even became dirty so there was no chance I could make M happy that way. Not to mention I couldn't go out and make money, because M was the one who found you the boys. She had been sending Katherine out every day, and she would be gone for hours. Sometimes M would go with her, but mostly M went out by herself. That meant that it was me and Kitty stuck in the house together all day every day.

Kitty was so perfectly flawed. I had never seen anyone as skinny as her, you could almost see every bone in her body and the way they contoured her body was more interesting and different than gross. I didn't speak much around her.

She came up to me one day, when we were alone in the house. "Hi." She said, it was always a surprise when she spoke. "Hi Kitty." I said with a smile. "You could ask M" she said, and I had no idea what she meant. You would think my confused face would have given it away, but Kitty continued to stare at me waiting for my response. "Ask M for what?" I asked after she didn't elaborate on her own. "Oh." She said I guess she realized she wasn't very clear. "For a boy." She said. "Why would I do that?" I asked even though I knew the answer, I wanted to impress M and I knew that would be the best way. Not to mention I was so bored. "Katherine had to ask." She said and I nodded. That makes sense, how would she know that I wanted a boy if I didn't ask? Of course, why else would I be here if I didn't want a boy? Kitty stayed in the room for a while, and I wasn't sure what to say. I wanted to ask her to lay with me. That's the type of person Kitty was. The one you wanted to hold and love, not talk too. I didn't ask her though, and eventually she left the room.

CHAPTER THIRTEEN

I decided to ask her that night. I was hoping we could have another one of our one-on-one talks once everyone was asleep. I had thought about what I was going to say all day. Kitty was being very clingy with M, or maybe I was noticing it more since I wanted some alone time with her. Katherine was still out, she had left early that morning. I had heard her get out of bed and get dressed as quietly as she could. Thankfully she had gone back to sleeping in the room with me, but she wouldn't talk to me still.

Eventually it was getting late, and I knew I had to say something. "M?" I asked, while we were in the living room. She nodded letting me know she heard me. "Could I talk to you?" this got her attention. "What?" She said. "I was wondering if I could get a boy." I asked and I felt like maybe I didn't word it right. "Like, what Katherine does. Maybe I could do it too. I could give you the money since I've been staying here a lot." That sounded a little better. She thought about it, "Are you sure?" she asked, but it wasn't a question to make sure I was okay with the idea, it was a question of whether I was sure I could handle it, whether I was sure I was good enough. "Yes." I said.

The next day I woke up before Katherine, I hadn't even heard her come in, but there she was in bed with all of her clothes on. She must have been really tired. I went into the living room so I wouldn't wake her up, and I saw M there. "I got someone for you." She said, and handed me the paper with an address. "I go here?" I asked "yes." She said, "don't be late, you have to be there in an hour." I wondered how she knew I would be awake in time to get there in an hour.

The entire walk there I tried not to think about anything. The apartment was small, smaller than M's for sure. I knocked on the door, and a guy answered. He was older than Mark, maybe in college? He asked if I was Coco and I nodded. He let me in and led me towards his bedroom. Once we were in there I had no idea what to do. I tried to think of Mark, and what I would do if it was him. I took off my shirt, which was kind of a big deal. It was very brave move and apparently even he thought so. He looked me up and down and grinned this half grin that made him look mischievous "Lay down." I said, and he sat on his bed. I got on his lap and took off my bra.

It hurt less than it had with Mark, which was good. It was less empowering though, I don't know why. I was proud of myself for being able to do it, and I couldn't wait to give Katherine details and see if it made M any less mad at me. But this boy meant nothing to me, and I could feel that I meant nothing to him. There was no connection, and I'm not saying me and Mark had this amazing love connection when we hooked up, but we had gone on dates and that made it more personal. It was obvious this guy was focused on himself, and not me. He was more experienced than

Mark, which is probably why it hurt less, or maybe I was just getting used to it. I tried to remember to ask Katherine about that. If she would talk to me.

When he was finished he didn't ask me to stay, in fact he looked at me like he was ready for me to leave. I got dressed and then wondered about the money. Was I supposed to ask? Did he already know? Maybe he already paid M? I remember the way Katherine's guys just handed her the money, and I was irritated that this guy didn't. "I need the money." I said, and he handed me $25. It wasn't the fact that he thought what we did was only worth $25 that upset me, it was that I knew M would not be happy with $25. I would have to do what I just did at least a couple times a day to even make enough to make her happy. I knew she said it wasn't about money for her, but I also knew she wasn't happy with me and I had to do my best to change that. The only way I knew how was to do this, and here this guy was ruining my chance by only giving me $25.

When I got back Katherine was awake in the room, she looked so tired. Nobody else was home, so I was excited to talk to her. "Are you still mad at me?" I asked, and she gave me a look that answered my question. "I did it, M got me a boy and I made some money." I said, hoping she would be able to put her anger aside for a bit. She smiled at me, and I knew she could. "How much?" was the first question she asked, and instantly I felt upset. "Only $25" I said and she shrugged like it wasn't a big deal. "It wasn't like when I was with Mark." I said and she nodded like she understood. "You'll get used to it" she said and that helped. She hugged me and I could tell that we weren't fighting anymore. "Thank you" I said.

M got home later, and I stayed awake for her. She walked in and looked right at me, then she walked straight to her room. Even Katherine looked at me confused. I thought she would want to talk to me, I thought she would want to know how it went. I know this wasn't a big deal for them but I wasn't them. This was my first time. A few seconds later she came back into the living room. "How did it go?" she said. "It was fine" I said, even though it was only M and Katherine in the room I suddenly felt insecure. "Just fine?" she asked "It was good. What should I do with the money?" I asked. "Just keep it" she said and she walked back into her room. I felt like I had let her down. Why was M always so cold? Why couldn't she love me like she loved Kitty or even Katherine? Why wasn't I worth that to her?

M was gone the next day, that meant that Katherine, Kitty and I were in the house alone. It was boring, and I kind of wished M would have given me a boy to go to. Kitty kept to herself as always while Katherine and I talked about everything. We were becoming really good friends, and I felt bad not including Kitty but I didn't know how. It seemed like Katherine didn't either, she ignored Kitty most of the time and Kitty ignored her. For someone who was so clingy with M, she sure was independent when she was with anyone else. Sometimes I wanted to talk to her, but I could never find the right words.

It was getting late when M got home, I could tell Katherine was starting to get nervous and Kitty looked more sad than usual. I think M probably told them she would be home before they went to bed and since it was getting late they started to get restless, thinking that she wouldn't. But M always kept her promises, you could rely on her. That's why you loved her. "Hi girls" she said when she got home, her voice was softer than it usually was. She sat on the floor where Katherine and I were sitting, and Kitty walked over from the wall she had been leaning against. Kitty now had a smile on her face. She looked so pretty when she smiled. I loved Kitty too. M's eyes were watery, so I thought that maybe she had been crying. "Hi" Katherine said and Kitty put her hand on top of M's, she was still smiling despite M's watery eyes.

"I love you" she said to no one in particular, but it felt like she was speaking to each of us individually. I know it probably wasn't possible, but it felt like she was looking at each of us when she said it. Like her words held more power than they did, like that I love you had a million stories, apologies, compliments and heartache packed into each word. It was a strong I love you, not the one you say out of habit. It felt like the first I love you that you say in a relationship, that you think about for weeks and wonder if it's too early to say but eventually the feelings you have for them are so strong you blurt it out. It felt like the I love you that you say when you really messed up, where it might be the last time you say those words to that person and you want to make sure they sound right.

None of us said it back, not because we didn't love her but because we did. This was her moment, she was feeling something and we wanted to experience it with her. If we spoke, if we said we loved her back the moment could be over. We all knew there was no way we could tell her we loved her the way she just told us she loved us.

"I haven't been prefect." She said, now she was looking at Kitty, then me, then she looked at Katherine. I wanted to look at Katherine, but I couldn't stop looking at M, couldn't stop listening to her. I didn't care what caused this change in her. I couldn't decide whether I liked it or not. I wanted her to be strong, to protect us. I think in doing so though, she became mean at times. She loved us though, and no matter what she did from this point on I knew she loved me. Nothing she could ever do would take away the words she had said, the love she had for me in her eyes that was nothing like I had ever seen. "You're more than my friends" she continued, "You're my sisters." She squeezed Kitty's hand while looking at me. I smiled and so did she.

She turned towards Kitty and said "You are the most beautiful girl. You are perfection." She kissed her forehead, and I saw a tear run down M's face. I felt hurt, I wanted to be beautiful to M. I knew I couldn't compete with Kitty though. M's compliments were real, which made them mean more. She turned to Katherine, who seemed to be waiting for her turn. They looked at each other for a moment then M said "You are so strong." Then she kissed her forehead. If I was Katherine I would have been upset. I would rather be beautiful than strong. She turned towards me last, and for a second I was scared that I would miss it. The words she had said to Kitty and Katherine were so short. "You're going to be like me one day." She said.

CHAPTER FOURTEEN

The next day was peaceful and happy. It felt like summer, the air was warm but not heavy, and everyone in M's house wore a smile. Even Kitty. M was in a relaxed mood and we were talking more freely to one another. I wanted another boy, but I thought I would wait until later to ask. M's words the day before had stuck with me. I didn't know what she meant. They had more meaning in them and felt like so much more of a compliment than what she had said to Kitty or Katherine. I don't know if either of them realized it though. It seemed like they were more content with their own words from M that they didn't see the ones I had, that made it more special though.

"So I was thinking" M said "You should go home today and spend some time with your dad." I was not expecting that. But I wasn't about to argue either. "Um. Okay." I said then after a few moments asked "why?" she smiled and sat next to me. "Well, I was thinking you should spend a few days with him." My face must have mimicked what I was feeling because M quickly added "I was hoping you could move in for the summer, maybe even longer." I smiled, big. There was no hiding it or pretending to be cool about it. I was smiling so big that my face was hurting, and that made M laugh harder than I ever heard her laugh.

That night she walked me home, she knocked on my door, which was kind of weird because I lived there but I wasn't going to question her. My dad answered the door and looked confused as to why we had knocked. "Hi, I'm M. Coco and I went to school together last year and she had been staying at my house for a few days." She extended her hand for a handshake, which was way more formal than any teenager has ever been with my dad. "Wow, you're polite." My dad said and looked at me in a way that said he was impressed.

I walked into the house and motioned for M to come inside. "So, you go to school together?" My dad asked even though M had already said that. "yeah, I just graduated this year." M said, and I looked at her confused. Didn't she say earlier that she was dropping out of school? Well, I guess it would sound better to my dad. "That's nice, so where do you live?" my dad asked, typical dad always asking the obvious questions. The problem with all of this was he was clueless. No matter how many questions he asked, he was absolutely clueless. He didn't understand how teenagers really were. He didn't understand me.

"I actually live in my own apartment" she said "I live there with our two other friends-Katherine and Kitty. They both go to school with Coco too." My dad looked impressed again, I never really had many friends before and now I had three. Surprise! "That's actually what I wanted to talk to you about dad" I said trying to jump into the conversation, and get it over with. "Katherine and Kitty live with M during the summer, and I was hoping you would let me move in too." My dad looked like he wasn't sure "Just for the summer" I quickly added. "Well...I don't know" my dad said, I could almost feel him wanting to check his stack of parenting books for 'what to do when your daughter wants to move into her friend's house that you have only met just now'.

"I understand if you're not comfortable, but the way Coco made it sound was that she was going to be eighteen soon and she wanted to learn some independence before she became officially an adult. You understand how it was when you were a teenager." M talked to my dad like they were friends. My dad nodded his head slowly in agreement, but he still looked unsure. "It would only be until school started back up again." M said, but it sounded more final like M decided I would be living with her and there was nothing my dad could say. I didn't think it would work, but my dad looking uneasy said "Okay. Well it sounds like fun."

I was supposed to stay at my dad's house for a few days, but he insisted that I go back to M's. The summer was short he said. I was so excited to be able to be with them all the time, moving in meant I was becoming more a part of their group.

M had me and Katherine go together when we met our boys. We had about two each every day which I liked, it was better to have what Katherine called a "warm-up guy. The first boy you were with was always worse than the second, no matter how many boys you hooked up with you always seemed to go back to that shy, uncomfortable girl with the first boy of the day. After you were done with him and got the money and of course the compliments you had a lot more confidence. M always hated when we referred to the first boys as the warm up guys. "All of them should get equal attention girls" she would say, but she was never serious. She always said it with a smile that she tried to hide. M would try to arrange the times we met our boys close together, but sometimes there would be a gap and those were the times I loved the most. Katherine and I would lay on the grass and talk about everything. I may have looked up to M but Katherine and I had the closest relationship. We understood each other, we shared so much. We both loved M with every inch of our body, and there is something special about sharing love. I guess it must be that way when parents have a child, it brings them closer because they both love the same person. They understand the need to protect them and make them proud of you. You can have the same favorite color as your friend or want to study the same thing in college but none of that stuff matters, none of that stuff gives you an unbreakable bond. Being able to have someone who is doing the same things that you are doing every day, striving to be the best person they can be, that's a shared journey that sisters share. I couldn't imagine my life without her. I thought sometimes that she was as thankful for me as I was for her. I wondered if she was lonely before me, with Kitty being so withdrawn and M's distance. When we were all together, Katherine, Kitty, M and me, I could see Katherine get more guarded, she was more thoughtful about the words she said. But when it was just us, laying on the grass in the sun waiting for the next boy, I saw the happiness in her. She smoked cigarettes and I would watch the smoke travel up into the sky. She had a smile that was bigger than anyone I've met and she had a great sense of humor. She was young.

I know the happiness comes from M and the lifestyle she gave to Katherine. M gave us both a life we would never be allowed to have without her. We both would be stuck. I would be in a boring, meaningless life. Katherine would be on a self-destructive path. I don't know Kitty's story, but she seems so lost even around M that I know whatever life M took her from must have been awful.

CHAPTER FIFTEEN

"Do you think you'll ever find love?" I asked, not to anyone in particular, maybe I meant the question to all of the girls. We were lying on the floor, for no reason, staring at the ceiling. It was something we did, something strange that most people don't do. We relaxed a lot, we didn't talk much, but we loved each other more than anything. These girls were making me into who I was, they were supporting me during the process, they loved me deeply, and I knew when it was all over I would be a part of their group. With all of us laying there- my head on the floor but Katherine's hand brushing against mine. Kitty's head on M's shoulder but Katherine's arm around her. And M's presence protecting all of us, making all of us different girls into a group that worked. "I think the question is will we ever want to find love?" Katherine replied. "I already found love." Kitty said and I could feel M smiling even though I couldn't see it. "I think we all have." M said.

CHAPTER SIXTEEN

One day M told us that we would not be going together. Katherine had boys lined up, she would have five boys so she would be out all day. I could see the overwhelmed look in her eyes. Katherine might have been experienced and I knew she loved the feeling of being in control of these boys but whenever she had more than two she got overwhelmed. There was a fear that you wouldn't be able to fit all of them in one day. You could never time how long each guy would take, so it was kind of a guessing game. M would not be happy if we didn't get to all the boys she planned for us. Not to mention it physically wears you out, I remember one day Katherine complained about being sore and I joked that the boys were helping her keep her great body. She laughed, but the more I thought about it the more I thought that it was more truth than joke. M told me that I had two guys, but that they were a couple of hours apart. "Should I come home between them?" I asked but she shrugged to let me know she didn't care.

The first guy was great. He was probably the most attractive guy I had been with yet. He was experienced too, I actually almost enjoyed it. He paid me $50 and complimented my hair. He wrapped it up in his hand and tugged it. He kissed my neck and told me he would be requesting me again. This was the first boy who ever said he would ask for me again. I knew Katherine had a few repeat boys, but she told me they were hard to find. Most boys did this as a one-time thing, something to try out. The ones who did it frequently didn't want to get attached to one girl. "What's the point?" Katherine said one day "Why hook up with the same girl over and over again? You can get that for free, it's called a relationship." M overheard us and added "No, a relationship costs way more than you girls."

I couldn't wait to get home and tell M. I knew she would be proud of me. Repeat guys always paid more. This was a big deal! I was bringing in a couple hundred a week, and Katherine brought home double what I did. Sometimes that made me feel bad, but she reminded me that she had been doing this a year more than I had. M never brought up the money but I knew she needed it. None of us had a real job, but we had real expenses. I felt accomplished to be finally making some progress, and I knew M would be too.

I walked up to the door and it was unlocked, M didn't give anyone a key but she left the door unlocked most times. Maybe it's shock, or maybe it's denial. I stood there, staring. I knew what I was looking at but my brain didn't register it. I was looking right at them, but I didn't put it together. I stood there for a few minutes, taking the scene in. M looked directly into my eyes, she was determined. Her eyes weren't mean or even passionate, they were just determined. Motivated. She didn't say anything but maybe that's because I didn't let her. I ran. I ran out of the door and didn't bother to shut it. I ran fast and I ran far. I ran until my lungs felt like they couldn't get any more air in.

I sat on the sidewalk, well I sort of laid on the sidewalk. I tried to collect myself. What did I see? M. I saw M in the living room, she was naked. Completely naked. Her body looked different than I imagined. She looked like a women, I knew she had curves but not like that. She looked older. Different. I saw two guys. I had never met them before. They were naked too. On the living room, M with two naked guys. I closed my eyes. I shouldn't have ran. I seemed to be relaxing, and my thoughts seemed to be finally putting it together. I knew why I ran.

It was Kitty. She was next to M, naked. With the two guys touching her, too rough. They were too rough with her. She was so small, so fragile, so weak, so simple. M should have stopped them. Kitty wasn't there, but she was there. Her eyes had a faraway look, like she didn't even understand what was going on. They looked sad. Her eyes always looked sad I tried to remind myself. Kitty didn't look like she should have been there. Unlike M, she looked exactly like you would have thought she would look naked. Her bones poked out at every angle, they were grey. Her skin was white. Her hair was silver. Her eyes were grey,.. and so sad. "This is what we do" I said out loud to myself. No, this is what I do. This is what M does. This is what Katherine does. We do this. Not Kitty. Kitty can't do this. Kitty is the one who cleans and fills in the gaps when we all lay together. Kitty is the one who sits quietly in the room when everyone else is talking. I got up and started walking. At first I didn't know where I was headed, but then I realized I was walking towards my next guy. I was going to meet him and do what M and Kitty were probably still doing.

I did what I was supposed to, I did what was expected of me. I don't know why, maybe it was out of habit. Maybe I thought I could go home and nobody would mention what had happened. And then there was the money issue. I knew I needed to bring money. I was going to go back, of course, this wasn't like last time I left. I just needed some time to think. Maybe I was looking towards him to comfort me. Or maybe I just needed something to do until I figured out what I was going to do. I didn't stop thinking though, I couldn't stop thinking about what had happened. Kitty's body next to M's. The contrast was too shocking. I kept trying to figure out what I was thinking. I would think 'Kitty is just like us' and then I would think 'No she's younger. Much younger.' I would think 'I watched Katherine before there is no difference' and then I would think 'watching her is much different than being with her.'

The guy didn't seem too impressed with me, I understand that. I didn't even remember most of what happened. I got up and got dressed slowly, not caring about him complaining about how long it was taking me to leave. I felt like I was moving in slow motion, like my thoughts were slowing me down. I didn't care. I went outside and it was starting to get dark. I began walking and this time I really didn't have anywhere to go. I walked for hours, or I guessed it was hours. It was dark by the time I arrived at M's house. At this point I had convinced myself that I was okay with what happened. Kitty is old enough to make her own choices. She looked younger, but she's not. She is in high school, just like us. She knows what we do, she had too. We talked about it in front of her, why would I be so ignorant to not think that she did it as well? Why would M allow her as part of our group if she didn't? She told me I had to do this stuff to be their friend, so of course Kitty would have to as well. She was attractive too, it made sense that guys would want her. Why would M waste an opportunity like that? The more I thought about it the more it made sense. M was probably doing it with her to protect her. The thought was kind of the conclusion to my confusion. I felt satisfied with what I put together.

M was sitting on the couch. I knew this wasn't going to be good. Katherine and Kitty weren't anywhere, but I knew they were here. They probably were asleep, I hoped they were asleep. I sat on the couch next to M, but we didn't look at each other. We both looked the wall in front of us. There was a lot of silence and I wondered if I should speak, if speaking would get this over with sooner. Before I could decide M said "Why did you leave, again." The emphasis she put on the word again made me look down at the floor. She was disappointed in me. She might even have been angry with me. "I'm sorry" was all I could say, I was scared if I said anything else it would be the wrong answer. She grabbed my arm and turned me towards her. She was angry. Her fingers dug into my skin, and the pain caused something in me. I might have been angry too.

"That's. Not. An. Answer." She said, or rather she muttered. She was speaking so quietly I could only hear her because there was no other noise in the house. I yanked my arm from her grasp and she looked surprised. "I was shocked. Okay? Am I not allowed to be shocked?" she shook her head, she had less anger on her face and more of a look that said 'I should have known.' I looked down again. "You should think before you speak." She said a little louder now. She had told me this over and over again, she shouldn't have had to tell me it over and over again. "I'm sorry" I muttered, because it was safe. It was a safe phrase. I would take her anger over her disappointment any day.

She stood up and walked to the other side of the room, which was pointless, but I guess she had to get up and do something. Maybe sitting down was making her anger worse. "I thought you were different" she said and the words beat into me. "I'm sorry" I said again this time so quiet I knew she wouldn't be able to hear it. I was like a child getting lectured by her parent. My head hung and I hoped it would end soon. "Do you know how you made Kitty feel?" she said and that was what brought the tears. My eyes got blurry, but I refused to blink knowing if I did my face would be flooded with tears. I had thought about Kitty the entire day, but I never thought about how me running out might make her feel. "No" I said "She was sad. She thought she did something wrong. She thought you were grossed out by her. We cannot be like that. We are sisters. We love each other. That's why I make all of us do this, because if only Katherine and I did everyone else would feel left out. There would be a gap. We wouldn't understand each other the way we do" She sat back on the couch and held my hand. The tears wanted to fall, but I held them back. I thought that if I cried she would feel obligated to comfort me, and although I wanted her comfort more than anything at that moment I didn't feel like I deserved it. "Can I talk to her?" I asked, and I meant it. I wanted to talk to Kitty for the first time. I wanted to talk to her like a friend, something I never did before. She stood up again. "No. You can't, she's asleep. But I do expect you to apologize to her tomorrow." I nodded. "Go get dressed for bed Coco. Then come back out here." I got up and went into the room. Katherine was sitting on the bed, awake and obviously listening to everything that was happening. It was dark though and I couldn't read the expression on her face, but maybe that was best. I got undressed and remembered the money I had in my pocket.

I came back into the living room and handed M the money, she took it without saying anything. "I got a repeat." I said quietly. She looked impressed and I wanted to smile, but I couldn't. This wasn't the time. "That's good. How?" she asked, and I told her about the guy, and how he told me he was pleased with me and that he would tell her he wanted me again. Her face stayed neutral but her words sounded proud. "I knew you could do it." She said. "That's why I don't understand how you could do what you did." I deserved that. I looked down again. "You should have joined." She said. I had not expected that. "What?" I asked, making sure I heard her right. "You should have joined us when you walked in. The guys were insulted. They know me and they know what we do. They saw you run out and they thought it was them. We will probably never make money off of them again because of you." I couldn't believe what she was saying. I felt bad about causing a scene, I did. I was wrong for that. I felt bad about Kitty, that was horrible of me and I wanted to make it up to her. But I was new to this, it was a shock to see them like that. How could I have just joined them? Not to mention I couldn't imagine being naked and doing that with M watching, and definitely not Kitty! Katherine was one thing, they were another.

What I said next was stupid, and it proves that M is right about thinking before you speak. "Are you serious?" I said "I don't have to join you! I shouldn't have to! I was shocked. You were naked! Kitty was naked! There was two guys!! What did you expect me to do M? I'm not like you!!" I was screaming now, and next thing I knew I was on the floor. She had slapped me, hard. My cheek burned and my body hurt from the fall. I thought Katherine was strong, but M was apparently pretty strong too.

I didn't get up. I was scared she would slap me again. I should never have talked to M that way. "You are just like us." She wasn't yelling, but this was worse. "If you don't want to be like us leave now." She said I could leave, but her voice was saying otherwise. I knew I couldn't leave.

"Go to bed." She said and I got up and went into the room. Katherine was asleep, or at least pretending to be asleep. I laid in bed, wide awake, staring into the darkness. I

thought about M, Kitty, Katherine, I thought about me. I
knew I made a mistake, I just didn't know what it was.

CHAPTER SEVENTEEN

Katherine left before I even woke up, I know she probably didn't set it up that way, but I still felt like she was avoiding me. She knew I was in trouble with M, and she didn't want to be involved with that. We were all friends, but when someone was in trouble you stayed away from them. Katherine and I might have been close, but our loyalties were with M.

I was afraid to face M, but I was more afraid to face Kitty. I wanted to talk to her, to apologize but I also was scared to see her reaction. Nobody ever really talked to her except for M, so I didn't know what she would say. I got dressed slowly, trying to procrastinate. Eventually I knew I had to go into the living room, I could hear M talking but I didn't know what she was saying. I tried to decipher whether she sounded like she was in a good mood or not but it was hard to tell. I opened the door to see Kitty and M laughing on the floor.

Seeing them laughing actually made it harder. I didn't feel included, and I didn't have to ask if I was welcome to join in on the joke. M looked up at me and smiled, which meant she knew what I was feeling and she wanted me to feel that way. "Kitty?" I asked and she looked up at me, it's hard to imagine her being anything other than a breakable girl even though I saw her in a much different light yesterday. "I'm sorry about yesterday" I said, M was smiling even harder. She was loving this. Kitty nodded and shrugged. I couldn't tell if the shrug meant it was nothing, or that she didn't care about my apology. I looked at M to see if that was enough, or if I should say anything else. She too shrugged, imitating Kitty and making fun of me. Making this harder for me. She wanted me to feel ashamed. She wanted me to feel like I wasn't apart of the group. She tried to hold back a laugh, and I felt embarrassed. Didn't she see I was trying to make things right? "Kitty can we talk in private?" I asked but I knew it was no use. Kitty shook her head no, and M burst out laughing.

After she was finished laughing, she got up and told Kitty to go into the room. When it was just me and M I could really see how happy she looked. Too happy. "Do you have any guys for me today?" I asked and rolled my eyes, I was starting to get annoyed with her. We were supposed to be fighting and here she was in front of me smiling harder than ever. "Yeah I do." The way she said it made it seem like the sentence wasn't finished, like there should have been more. Like she had just told a joke but left out the punchline. "Okay.." I said confused. "I'm going with you." She said and everything stopped. I couldn't do that. I couldn't do what I did in front of M, I never even did it in front of Katherine. M was critical, and since we were fighting I knew she would be worse. I thought about leaving again. I guess M could tell because she said "If you ever leave this apartment again without asking you are done. I am done with you. You will never talk to me again. You will not talk to Kitty or Katherine. We will all be done with you, and you will go back to being the pathetic tease you were when I met you." Her words hurt, but her voice was calm, even light. "You will sleep with the boys in front of me until sex doesn't become uncomfortable for you. Until you learn what you're supposed to do. You will be working all day, every day until I say so." She ran her hand through my hair, and I closed my eyes. I wanted her to love me so bad.

We didn't go anywhere, we stayed in the apartment. M sat on Katherine's bed and I waited on mine. The first guy had to be in high school, he was scrawny and pale. He seemed a bit insecure with M watching and that added to my nervousness. I took my clothes off and felt M's eyes on me. I wondered if she was judging me, if she thought I was attractive or if she wondered why anybody would pay for me. If she was assessing me, trying to figure out if I was good enough for her. Once the boy saw that I was naked he seemed to catch on that he needed to get naked as well. This was going to be a long and drawn out process I could already tell, I was starting to wonder if he was a virgin. I looked over at M and once again she was smiling. Thriving in my misery.

It was as awkward as I had thought it would be. He didn't know what to do the entire time and when he was done he didn't leave. He just laid there, like he lived there. Thankfully M told him he had to leave. The next boy was at least attractive, and I was able to show off a bit more. I wanted M to know I could do this, I wanted to prove her wrong. After the first boy I was feeling more confident, but every time I looked over at her she seemed distracted. Of course. The first guy I'm good with and she's not paying attention.

I was starting to wonder how many guys I would have after the fourth one, Katherine had only had five at the most, so I was hoping that I would only have one more. I was wrong. I lost count after seven. I thought that I might have been losing consciousness because the guys seemed to blend together. My body was so sore, and maybe because I was in pain but it seemed like the guys became rougher. None of them cared, I thought I told one of them or maybe more than one that I needed a break. I pushed one of them off of me but he just came back. The room seems so dark and the air was so thick. I tried to turn on my side, maybe to get some sleep or maybe to get in a more comfortable position but I was forced to lay on my back.

Eventually my body knew I couldn't take anymore. I think I must have been crying because my face was wet and it was hard to see. I tried to get up but once again I was shoved down and when I hit the mattress it felt like I hit concrete. I yelled out for M, and she came over and made the guy leave. She looked at me, and shook her head. I don't know why I called out for her, she was the one who put me in that situation. No, I was the one who put me in that situation. I was lightheaded and tired. "You have a lot to learn." She said.

CHAPTER EIGHTEEN

Katherine came home later, I woke up when I heard her. I didn't say anything, but she saw me. I don't know what she saw though exactly, I didn't know how bad I looked. But she knew. I wondered if M told her what happened. She pulled the blanket over me and laid in bed with me until I fell asleep. Her body was warm, she wasn't soft like M or moveable like Kitty and on any other day I wouldn't have wanted to cuddle her. She didn't have that kind of body. She wasn't that kind of girl. I needed someone then though, and she was offering so I let her. I knew I didn't deserve it, I didn't deserve her comfort. I should have laid on that bed, feeling dirty and hating myself. She wouldn't let me though, she wouldn't let me beat myself up over what I did. Maybe she didn't know what I did.

The next morning I woke up and cried. I cried because I knew what was going to happened. I knew that I would have to repeat yesterday. I cried because my body was sore, and every movement hurt. I cried loudly, it was an embarrassing sob. I didn't care who heard me. I cried until my eyes refused to produce anymore tears. Then M walked in. I knew she has been listening to me, waiting until I was done. "Why were you crying?" she said and sat on the bed, she seemed impatient like she wanted to get this over with.

"I'm sad." I said, and I guess that was true. I mean I was crying, obvious I was sad. "Why?" she said, I knew what she was doing. She wanted to analyze my feelings, she wanted me to stop acting on emotion, and start making myself into a better person. "You're mad at me, and I don't want you to be." She looked at me expressionless. "Just do what I tell you to today." I nodded and wiped my face. "Don't bother getting ready" she said as she started making Katherine's bed. My hair had been plastered to the pillow and I knew my face must have been red from all the crying. I laid back down, I didn't care. I didn't care what I looked like to these boys, I only cared what M thought about me. Everyone else in the world didn't matter anymore. I needed her, and nobody else.

"How much longer?" I asked and she sighed "If you can get through today without asking me to make them leave then today will be the last day. If not we will continue every single day until you can." That was reassuring, I knew that all I had to do was get through today and things would be back to normal. "You won't hate me?" I asked hopefully. "Just worry about getting through today." She replied.

It was worse than the day before, much worse. I focused less on trying to impress her and more on getting through the pain. Because it hurt. Bad. I started to realize this wasn't about me showing her I could do it, this was a punishment. I don't know why I didn't get it before. She was punishing me for talking to her the way I did. She was punishing me for not joining in. I would never disrespect M again.

Boy after boy. They all seemed the same at that point. I didn't care about them, or what they did to me. I didn't know how much time passed but I was hoping it would be over soon, it was dark outside so I knew Katherine would probably be home soon. I hoped that meant I would be done.

One of the guys was rougher than the others. I didn't mention anything but I could see the look on M's face. She looked a little worried but she didn't stop him. Until he slapped me, when he slapped me she jumped off the bed and yelled at him to leave. I had never heard M yell before, and it was terrifying. I was so scared that I started to tremble. I wasn't scared of the guy, a slap was nothing compared to how my body felt. I was scared of M, she seemed so angry. I didn't think that she was protecting me, I just knew she was mad and I didn't want to be around that. Once he was gone, I waited for the next guy but nobody came. She left the room for a while and then came back. She pulled me close to her and kissed my cheek. "It's okay Coco" she said over and over again. She must have said it a hundred times. Maybe she could feel me shaking. For the first time I slept with M, she laid in my bed and held me the entire night. I slept better than I ever had before.

CHAPTER NINETEEN

Whenever you go to sleep one way and wake up another way it's a shock. You go to sleep expecting to wake up with things the same way. That's not how the world works though, just because your world pauses when you're asleep it doesn't mean everyone's does.

I woke up and M wasn't there. I knew I was in pain before I even moved, which made me too scared to move an inch. I laid there for a while until I convinced myself that I couldn't spend the remainder of my life in bed and that the pain I would feel from getting up was inevitable. I sat up slowly and my entire body ached. A sharp shooting pain ran up my leg and into me. I sat on the edge of my bed and realized something else was wrong. Something besides the pain I was feeling. Katherine was asleep in the bed next to me and I woke her up. I don't know why I woke her up, but I felt like she needed to be awake. Maybe I wanted to know if she felt the same way, like something was out of place. When I went to sleep M was next to me, holding me and things were good. When I woke up she wasn't there, and something about that felt wrong. Of course, she could have just gotten up because she woke up before me, but that didn't feel like the case. Something was wrong and I knew it. "Wake up Katherine!" I said after shaking her for a couple of seconds "What? What? What? What?!" she said her temper showing. "M's not here." I said and she opened her eyes "So?" she said and turned over. I gave up on her and walked into the living room, M was there but she was pacing. I knew something was wrong. "M?" I approached her carefully. "Kitty didn't come home." She said

"What do you mean Kitty didn't come home?" I asked as Katherine came into the living room looking irritated. She probably wasn't able to go back to sleep since I woke her up. "She went out last night to meet a guy and she never came home!" she was beginning to sound frantic "What's going on?" Katherine asked while pulling her hair into a ponytail "Kitty didn't come home" I said probably more calmly than would be expected. "What do you mean she didn't come home?" Katherine said asking the exact same question as me "She went out, she went out with a boy because I told her too. She went out and I didn't go with her." M said "You always go with her" Katherine said like it was a fact, like M had to be wrong. "I know!" M said, she kept pacing. "I was with you all night. I was with you and not her." She said and he words hurt. I knew this was about Kitty but it wasn't fair that she was ruining what M and I shared last night. That was a moment I held so close to me, something special we shared and now I knew M regretted it.

"I'm going out to look for her." She said "Should I go out? I have a boy I'm supposed to meet" Katherine said, obviously not concerned about Kitty "No!" she said and slammed the front door. Katherine sat on the couch and I sat on the floor in front of her. "Should we be worried?" I asked. "I don't know" she said, she seemed mad. "Are you mad?" I asked and it took her a while to answer, like she was thinking of what to say. "No. M is very protective of her though. I'm sure Kitty is fine."

She wasn't fine. She came into the house and I heard Katherine scream. Kitty laid on the floor, like she had struggled to get here and this was the place she needed to be. Like she ran a marathon and the apartment was the finish line. Her skin was no longer white, at least not anywhere I could see. It had bruises, if you could call them that- it was more accurately one giant bruise all over her body. Deep shades of black, blue, green and yellow. Her face was swollen and it made her look even younger, like she hadn't outgrown her baby fat yet. Her hair was wet, but I didn't know why. Her lip was swollen and bleeding, and her clothes were ripped. She was half-naked and I couldn't imagine how nobody stopped her. She was crying and she looked at Katherine "please.." she said. Katherine went to pick her up, and although weight wasn't an issue I could see that Katherine was trying to find a place to grab without hurting her. She placed Kitty on the couch and Kitty was crying harder. Katherine looked at me as if to ask what to do. I wasn't paying attention to her though, I was too busy assessing Kitty's injuries. That's when I saw it. Her arm was laying off to the side and her bone was sticking outwards. Her arm was broken. "We need to call the police" I said and Katherine looked at me like she couldn't believe what I had just said "No. We need M." Katherine said and she sounded scared. Katherine who you never would have thought could be scared a day in her life. Now it was my turn to look at her like I couldn't believe what she had just said. "Kitty is hurt. Look at her arm, it's broken. She is bruised all over. Her lip is almost completely gone. She is hurt, bad." Katherine seemed like she was taking what I said into consideration. "Well I don't have a phone" Katherine said so I grabbed mine and called the police.

I didn't know what to say when I called them. I mean what do you say when your friend gets beat up by some guy she was sleeping with for money? How do you tell the person on the phone that you're scared, not just for Kitty but for yourself? That you're scared your friendship was coming to an end? How do you tell them that you are only calling them because M is nowhere to be found? That you trust this girl over any police any day? How do you tell them how bad she looks? I could list all of her injuries but I wouldn't be able to describe the look in her eyes, the pain that was there. M didn't protect her. How do you tell the person on the phone that you hate the look on Kitty's face because it held judgement against M? How do you say that this is actually all your fault because you were getting punished while Kitty was all alone? You can't, so you don't. I only told them my friend was hurt. They came and took Kitty to the hospital in an ambulance. Which was what I wanted, what I didn't want was all the questions that came afterwards. "Who is Kitty?" "How old are you girls?" "Whose apartment is this?" "Where are your parents?"

"How did she get hurt?" I was getting overwhelmed. The police could tell and they separated Katherine and me. I couldn't hear what Katherine was saying but it looked like she wasn't saying much. I could tell because her lips weren't moving and the police that were talking to her looked mad.

"What's your name?" the female officer asked me, she wasn't pretty. Her hair was thin and pulled into a bun on top of her head. She wore little makeup but I think she might have actually benefited from some. I never wanted to be like her. "Coco" I said, again. I don't know why the officers didn't talk to each other and tell them what my name was. It seemed like every individual officer had asked me my name. "Kitty was the girl who was hurt?" and I nodded. "Coco I need you to tell me what happened." And I didn't answer, I stayed quiet and I thought. Just like M had taught me. Eventually I spoke "She came home and she was hurt." It wasn't a lie, but it wasn't everything I knew. I could have, and maybe should have, said 'Kitty was out with a guy having sex for money. She didn't come home last night like she should have so M went out and looked for her. A few minutes later Kitty walked in and she was hurt. We didn't even call the police for a while because Katherine wanted M. We were still protecting M.' But I didn't and I wouldn't. The female officer had walked over to talk to the officers talking to Katherine, I looked around the room there were five police officers there- two women and three men. None of the women were pretty, and I hoped the men would never contact M for us. They weren't attractive in the least.

The male officer stood beside me, guarding me, while the

other officers talked by Katherine. I hoped they wouldn't arrest us. "Wait home?" the female officer said when she came back over, I nodded. "You live here?" she said and I nodded again. She exchanged looks with the male officer. "Who else lives here?" she said now more nicely. The niceness made me nervous, the sudden change made me feel like I said something I shouldn't have. Like she pieced together too much information. If she was being nice that meant she knew I didn't hurt Kitty. Which is good, I thought. Did I really rather her think I hurt Kitty than her know what we did? "All of us" I said, and I didn't want to say anymore. I wanted to stay quiet. "You, Kitty, that girl over there.." she said listing everyone looking for my confirmation. I smiled when she said 'that girl over there' that meant that Katherine hadn't even told them her name.

They took us to the police station, but it wasn't like it was on the tv. It wasn't very dramatic. They wouldn't let me and Katherine near each other, but we weren't handcuffed or anything like that. They just put me in this room that looked like it could have been an office in my high school. It was nice being in there alone. I was able to think about what happened- Kitty was hurt. Really hurt. I wondered if she would be okay. Katherine was in another room, I guess, was she talking? No. Probably not. I hoped she wouldn't lose her temper with the police. I had no idea where M was, but I hoped she didn't come home. I didn't want the police to talk to her. I didn't want her to get in trouble. More importantly, I didn't want her to see Kitty hurt like she was.

I heard a tap on the door but nobody waited for me to say

come in, two women in suits opened the door and sat at the table. They looked serious but their features were softened. It looked so artificial. Like they always had stiff faces and they were trying too hard to appear kind. They sat down and introduced themselves- detective so and so. A few moments later my dad walked in, he looked uncomfortable, maybe even confused. He sat beside me without saying anything.

"What's your name?" the women said, she had brown hair. She was ugly too.

"Coco" I said, again, for the hundredth time that day.

"Hi Coco, are you okay?" the other women asked, she had short black hair. She was less ugly.

"Yes." I answered, I was determined to say as little as possible. I had called the police to help Kitty, which was done. I now had to protect me, M, and Katherine.

"Kitty is at the hospital" the ugly women said, and I nodded.

"We don't know if she is going to be okay." The less ugly women said slowly as if I wasn't understanding the significance of the event. She glanced at my dad, to see if he understood how serious things were. I doubt he did.

"Okay." I said, to let her know I heard her.

"What happened Coco?" the less ugly women asked and leaned in.

"Kitty came home hurt." I said and the ugly women looked at her papers she had in front of her and nodded

"You said home to the police officers but that's not where your father lives" she said and that's when my father spoke up "She is staying at her friend M's house for the summer." That was it, he ruined everything. I was trying to protect M and now that was ruined.

"Who is M?" the ugly women asked

I didn't speak. She glanced nervously at the less ugly women.

"Did you want to be there?' the ugly women asked me. I didn't understand her question.

"Of course I did!" I said, actually I kind of yelled. Which probably didn't make things better.

"Where did Kitty go?" the less ugly women asked, but it seemed like she knew the answer.

"I don't want to talk anymore. I want to see Kitty" that was the last thing I said to the detectives. They kept asking questions for a while but eventually they gave up and they told my dad that he could take me to the hospital but that they wanted me to come back first thing in the morning.

He drove me to the hospital and didn't say anything. He dropped me off, and when I asked if he was coming in he said no and told me to come back to his house when I was done.

Katherine wasn't there. Nobody was there. I thought that maybe Kitty's parents had come and were in the room with her. Maybe M had never came home, maybe she was still looking for Kitty. Maybe she had no idea what was happening. I sat down and waited. I don't know what I was waiting for, but I knew I wouldn't be able to see Kitty. The nurse probably would only let family in. Plus what if her parents were in there? I didn't know what to say to them. I sat back and closed my eyes, what had happened? I couldn't stop thinking about Kitty and how hurt she was. I tried not to, but I thought about some big guy beating her. I thought about her crying, I had never seen her cry before. I wondered if she had called out for M, even though she knew M was nowhere around. Just as I thought this I saw M walk in, she looked composed. Which made me feel better. It made me feel like maybe everything was okay. I stood up immediately and walked to her, she looked at me and wrapped her arms around me. "Coco" she said, she almost gasped my name. "M" I said in reply. She held my hand and walked me towards the nurse station. "I'm here to see Kitty Brown" she said it was odd hearing Kitty having a last name. I guess everyone had a last name though. "Who are you?" the nurse asked M without looking up from her paperwork on the desk. "We're her sisters. M and Coco" the nurse nodded and told us what room Kitty was in.

I didn't think about telling the nurse I was Kitty's sister, they would have let me in. That's why we relied on M so much. When we entered the room it was worse than when Kitty came home. She was cleaned up, which made her look less of a mess, but with that it also showed off all her wounds. Her arm was broken and in a cast. Her head was wrapped up in bandages, so I guess she had a head injury. I didn't even see any head injury before. Her lip was swollen way worse than it had been that morning. Her bruises were still there, prominent. I guess there was nothing the doctors could do about it. Her eyes were closed, and I hoped she was asleep. She had to be asleep if she was in the hospital. She's safe now, I tried to reassure myself. M picked up the clipboard that they kept at the end of the bed. She looked it over and tossed it on the bed, it hit Kitty's leg and I winced. I wondered if that hurt her. Probably not, she didn't move.

M walked over to me and we both stared at Kitty. She looked bad, she looked hurt. Yet she still had her look to her- that 'Kitty look'. Sad, young, beautiful, fragile. Even though she survived all of these injuries she still looked fragile.

"My parent's adopted her." M said and I didn't think I heard her right "What?" I asked "A couple of years ago.. Kitty was ten and I was fourteen. I guess it was some foster care type program or whatever, but they adopted her. She may have been ten but she was so small, you would have sworn she was younger. She was distant and she had such a sad look to her that it was hard to be around. I didn't talk to her much, I was too busy doing my own thing. I had a lot of boyfriends at the time." I couldn't imagine M having boyfriends. "One day I was having sex with my boyfriend in my bedroom and Kitty walked in, she didn't seem phased she just went over to my closet and got a shirt and walked out. My parents always told her she could wear my clothes. I couldn't believe that this young, small girl would be so comfortable around sex. That night I brought her into my room and we talked. We talked for hours." I couldn't imagine Kitty talking to anyone for hours. "She wanted a sister, she wanted a friend. My parents weren't very attentive. They did things that made them look good. Kitty needed more than they could give her. So, I loved her. We ended up sleeping in the same room at night, she followed me around everywhere, she did stuff for me cleaning and stuff like that, and she even started dating one of the guys I was with. I knew about it, and I didn't mind. In fact it was what gave me the idea to start sleeping with boys for money. I told Kitty about it one day and she agreed, she always agreed with me. When I was seventeen my parents walked in on me and Kitty with a few guys and they kicked us out. Well they kicked me out, they threatened to 'send Kitty back' I didn't even know where she would go. I told them I would take Kitty with me and they allowed it. We haven't talked to them in almost two years." I thought about this, and I realized how wrong it was of me to run away when I saw them. "I'm sorry" I said and I meant it. I was sorry for what had happened to her and Kitty, I was sorry that I had called the police and maybe gotten her in trouble, I was sorry that I had ran away when I saw them, I was sorry that M had to punish me and Kitty got hurt in the process. M nodded her head and ran her fingers over Kitty's swollen face. "I love you Kitty" she said but Kitty didn't acknowledge her. Kitty didn't move. I wondered if Kitty would ever be able to say it back.

M left the hospital and she didn't come back. I stayed overnight, I didn't sleep though, I just watched Kitty. The next morning I knew I had to go home, I knew my dad would have to take me back to the police station. Just as I was about to leave Katherine walked in. She looked nothing like she normally did, her hair was done and she had some makeup on. She wore an expensive dress and she looked awful. Even with the makeup her eyes were red from what I assumed was her crying. Her parents were behind her, and they looked upset. "Katherine!" I said and ran over to her, I could feel her parent's glares on us. "Is she okay?" Katherine asked in a soft voice, in a voice I never heard come out of her. "I don't know" I said and she looked down. She couldn't look at Kitty. She couldn't look at me. "What's wrong?" I asked Katherine. "They are making me move. I can't stay with M anymore. I can't see any of you anymore." Her voice came out in a plea, like I would be able to change the way things were. "Katherine.." I said. What would I do without her? She had become the closest thing to a friend I ever had. She walked out with her parents, and that was the last time I ever saw Katherine.

The next couple of days were a blur, the police asked me questions, and my dad avoided me as much as possible. Then the news stations caught on to the story and it was everywhere. The phone was always ringing and the few times I watched the news I heard phrases like "trafficking" and "troubled teens". I didn't say much to the police, and apparently neither did Katherine. I don't know if they questioned M, but I doubted they could get anything out of her either because the police eventually stopped asking questions. Kitty got better, slowly. I was the only one who came to visit her. When she finally woke up, she looked confused. Like she didn't know who I was. "Where's M?" was the first thing she said and I cried.

Kitty left the hospital, and I guess she went back into the system. I hoped some other family would adopt her, but I knew even if they did it wouldn't be M. And Kitty needed M.

Katherine moved, and I never heard from her again. I wondered if she was living extravagantly and if she was able to control her temper without M's help. But I knew that she hated her parents, and nobody could give her the life M gave her. Katherine needed M.

M left, I didn't know where she went, I don't think anybody did. I thought about her often, about her living a regular life or maybe she had found a new group of girls and was doing the same thing. That thought was the one that made me stay in my room for days and cry. Because I knew that M needed girls.

CHAPTER TWENTY

They asked me to talk. Everybody wanted me to talk. It's strange when you go from one extreme to another, when you're taught something is right and then expected to do the opposite. It wasn't until everyone was asking me to talk that I realized how silent I had been. It made me question whether I was always a quiet person or if I had become this way and if so when? I had learned to keep thoughts in my head, to think about every word I was going to say. The less you spoke, the more meaning the words you did say had. I believed that, even with all the people asking, begging, pleading, bribing, and even forcing me to talk. I had to think about my answers to their questions, had to work them so they came out correct and poised.

I wasn't covering for anyone, not for them and certainly not for myself. There was no point anymore. I stayed quiet for a long time, so I'm not sure what changed when the local news station asked me to talk. How was an under budgeted small-town news station any more important than my dad, or the police? They weren't. They called my dad, and asked if I could come in for a short segment to help "enlighten the world about what happened." When my dad quoted that it made me laugh, something I hadn't done in a while, regardless of what I chose to say the world would not be enlighten. For one, it was a local news station which meant that maybe ten percent of the people in a town of less than ten thousand would watch it.

But most importantly, no matter what I said or didn't say nobody would understand. They would never be able to understand the love we had for each other. I didn't even understand, not that I tried. Reason left with the girls. Even with all of this I told my dad I would do it, I would talk to the station about what I knew. Which, of course, was way more than they were expecting.

I'm not really sure what convinced me, all I knew was when I was sitting in that silver chair with the bright white lights shining in my face I was determined to tell every disgusting detail.

The women made me nervous- which made me uncomfortable- which made me feel guilty. Negative emotions are okay, it just depends on how you show them. Sadness could come off as beautiful, however being desperate or hysterical was annoying. Nobody wanted to be around someone who sobbed, but a young woman with tears streaming down her face was inviting. An invitation for comfort and love. Everything had to be thought out, even the way you felt. If you thought you felt some way you had to figure out why and how it could benefit you.

I tried not to fidget in my seat, I knew the cameras would be rolling soon and I wanted to appear calm and collected. If I seemed worried people might be more focused on that than my words. The women smiled down at me, which I suppose was a hint that we were going to be starting soon. She was pretty, but not in the way I was used to. She was pretty because she tried to be, she had on modern form fitting clothes that clearly were more expensive than she could afford, and her hair was slick and cut in a prefect angle barley touching her shoulder. I imagined her dreaming of being a big time news women in New York City. Obviously her dreams didn't work out. She was beautifully mature and sophisticated. We never utilized that imagine.

While most girls our age were trying to look older we were trying to look younger, or I guess at least close to our age.

Whether we believe it at the time or not, youth is beauty. So instead of trying to use makeup and clothes to grow us up too fast, we avoided all of that and focused on the features we were born with. "Natural beauty is the firmest form of attraction" I could almost hear M's voice in my ears as I examined the news woman in front of me. M made sure we never wore a lot of makeup, that our clothes were simple and showed our best parts, we let our hair fall naturally and left it untouched.

Regardless of all of this, we were still gorgeous. She held our appearances up to such high standards, but expected us to be beautiful without trying. Sometimes I think that she picked girls like us because we were born naturally pretty, I can't believe the women sitting in the chair next to me would have been able to pull off what we did wearing no makeup. However, I suppose before I never would have thought I could be like those girls either. They were flawless, and I was average.

Kitty was the youngest, so she had the easiest time, she was too young to gain weight or have acne. Her body was slim and pale, her hair was long and matched her white skin almost perfectly. Her eyes were a stormy grey that always seemed like they were on the verge of tears. She was short and the outline of her bones were the only curves she had developed. She was the prettiest by far, she was also M's favorite. Opposite of Kitty was Katherine, her body was toned and her light brown skin accented her long straight black hair. M was everything she hated in other girls, she had the body of a woman, and she was tan and blonde and had blue eyes. But she had so much confidence in herself that you had to believe she was the most gorgeous girl in the world.

"You're really beautiful" were the first words out of my mouth to the news woman- she smiled politely at me again and started shuffling her papers. "I used to be pretty too. But not like you. I was a different kind of pretty" The woman was taken back, I instantly regretted saying anything but I felt like I had too. This is why I'm supposed to think about what I say. But I did think about it, I was about to tell her that I was one of them, and I knew she wouldn't believe me with how I looked now. It had only been two weeks since the police talked to us, but I wasn't the same person. My blonde hair had faded and was thinning out. I wasn't getting the sleep I normally did, so my eyes were red and puffy.

I was snapped out of my thoughts when the reporter cleared her throat and announced that we were about to start. My heart started to race and I looked down at my jeans. If I was going to say anything now would probably be the right time. I'm sure once the cameras started rolling they would start asking their questions- questions that I didn't have the answers to. Such as "were there any warning signs?" or "if you had to guess was M really the ring leader?". I looked up at the women and said "I lied. I didn't know anything about those girls. I only hung out with them a few times." And I walked off the set.

I never got over M, Katherine and Kitty.

ACKNOWLEDGMENTS

I am so excited to have published my first novel! I have so many people to thank for their support, below are just a few of the people who have helped me. To everybody else, thank you for helping me accomplish this!

My wife, without the love and support of my wife Kendra I wouldn't have been able to publish this novel. Not only has she encouraged me along the way but she also came up with the title.

My family, I am so lucky to have a family who supports my dream of writing. I want to especially thank my mother for giving me my creativity and my father who encouraged reading throughout my childhood.

A special thanks to my cover model Whitney Sather, and my photographer Diane Brame. You guys did a great job!

ABOUT THE AUTHOR

Savannah Avery loves reading, writing, gardening, and all things related to homemaking. Girls is her first published novel. She lives with her wife in Virginia. You can visit her website at www.savannahavery.com

Made in the USA
Middletown, DE
06 July 2015